D0367547

BLAZING WEST

The Journal of Augustus Pelletier
The Lewis and Clark Expedition

★ KATHRYN LASKY ★

SCHOLASTIC INC.

ISBN 978-0-545-53084-2

12 11 10 9 8 7 6 5 4 3 2 1   14 15 16 17 18/0

Printed in the U.S.A.   40
This edition first printing, March 2014

The display type was set in Wells Grotesque Medium.
The text type was set in Berling.
Book design by Steve Scott
This edition photo research by Amla Sanghvi

Louisiana Territory
1804

May 20, 1804,
St. Charles, Louisiana Territory,
Missouri River, north bank

You ever see ink mixed up with blood? That's what's getting set down on this paper. It's my blood, too. No one else's. Came spouting out of my ear when Mingo pretty near sliced it off with his fish knife. I didn't cry then, and I didn't cry when I stitched it up myself tonight with the gut from the wildcat Mingo done shot. He'll probably try to cut my other ear off when he finds out I took that cat's gut. But he won't have a chance. I'll be gone. I decided tonight. I'm leaving.

I don't give a hoot what Captain Lewis and Captain Clark say. I don't care what my cousin Francis Labiche says—he's done been hired by them 'cause he speaks Omaha and is good with sign language. Well, I'm not half bad. Francis says I'm too scrawny, says "Hey, you don't weigh much more than a feed bag." I don't think size matters. Mama always said it didn't, not if you're a stand-up sort of fellow. Those were Mama's words for a right-doing man like my father. *Stand up.* Age shouldn't matter either. Still, Francis says I'm too young at fourteen. But one thing, I am unmarried. You can't be married to be part of the Corps of Discovery. That's what they call this outfit that's going up the Missouri all the way to the other sea at the very edge of this continent.

They are going at the special request of President Thomas Jefferson. And I'm going, too, whether they, or President Jefferson, want me or not. They're going in their big keelboat and two big flat-bottomed canoes, or pirogues, one white, one red. I'll be going on my own two blessed feet. I got my feet. Got almost two ears. Got my eyes. Got my sniffer. I can track anything. I'm just going to follow along the banks, through the woods, right out into the tall prairie grass. Sooner or later they're going to want me. And I ain't just running away from Mingo, although my stepfather be reason enough. I *want* to go. I want to know the hugeness of this land. I want to see the Big Water, the one they call the Shining Sea.

Later same night: My ear's hurting something fierce and I can't fall asleep. I don't worry none about Mingo coming back tonight. When he gets as drunk as he was tonight, he usually goes off for two, three days. So I thought I'd just sit up and write. Another hour it'll be dawn and I'll set out. I don't plan to go down to the landing. There'll be hundreds there to watch them set off. No, I'll get upstream a mile or so. Suddenly I see that I forgot to introduce myself. My name's Gus. Gus Pelletier. I'm half French, half Omaha Indian. My father, my real father, the one who helped birth me, was a trapper. He died before I could walk. My mother, Silverwing Woman, she was Omaha. She died last year. Mingo married her two years before. He came in full of promises and fancy talk. Soon as he got a woman to cook for him and a son to beat up he never worked another day so far as I could tell, or just enough to get his whiskey. I don't like to think too much about my mama.

This journal I'm writing in, my mother sewed it for me. Cut the covers from elk skin she had cured and worked. Got some paper from the priest here in St. Charles, Father Dumaine. Father Dumaine is the one who taught me how to read and write. St. Charles is a funny place, I guess. It's not more than twenty miles from St. Louis, but we don't have one-tenth the people. About four hundred of us all told. Mess of Indians. Mess of half-breeds like me, lots of French Canadians like Mingo and my father. A priest and a chapel. That's about it. So now you know me. Augustus Pelletier—half-breed, full-blooded American. Ready to go!

May 21, 1804

Oh, Lordy, I'm going to be able to run to the Shining Sea and back before this Corps gets off its lardy old butt and moves. I'd been waiting three miles upstream the whole day with no sign of them. Around four in the afternoon I ran practically all the way back to St. Charles and caught sight of them just a half mile out of the village. They must have started real late. Finally they made camp an hour ago just four miles up from where they began, on an island on the north side of the river. My mama and I had a name for this island. We called it Setting Down Goose Island. Those big old black and white geese used to set down and never move from it. It was like shooting fish in a barrel to get one for dinner, which we often did.

I got myself tucked in all cozy behind a willow break. They don't see me at all. I can see them. I can see their fires and smell their meat roasting. I'm not setting a fire. I took a big old hunk of venison from our larder. Got some jerky, too, and I done coal-baked half a dozen potatoes before I left. When that runs out I've got my fishing gear, and my father's old flintlock single-action rifle. Mingo will really pitch a fit when he finds it's gone. Come to think of it I'm in fine shape except for my ear. Doesn't hurt as much, but I'm scared to think what it's going to look like when I take the strapping rags off. I poured half a bottle of Mingo's whiskey on it, too. Mama told me that was the only good thing about whiskey—it could clean a cut. Mingo's really going to bust a gut when he sobers up and sees all I've taken. Of course, he's got part of my ear. But if I get to the Shining Sea I think it'll be a good trade.

May 22, 1804

They set off this morning at six o'clock sharp. I am most definitely faster than that big old keelboat and the pirogues, especially with the wind coming out of the west and hard on their nose. But it's not just the wind that's coming down on them. Bucketloads of junk are floating downstream—whole trees—cottonwoods, maples all uprooted from bank cave-ins—and when there's not a tree there are sandbars. Sometimes they get all snagged up. Then they have to break out the iron-spiked setting poles and pole their way around the tree or pry themselves off the sandbar.

Francis might think scrawny is bad, but I'm here to tell you that it's good. Darned if Francis didn't come within twelve feet of me on shore after they made camp and he was out shooting rabbits. I just slid myself behind a skinny cottonwood and he never even saw me. I'm just going to shadow this whole dang Corps all the way to the Big Water if I have to. I'll be the slimmest shadow that ever slipped through the grass. High noon when shadows are shortest they won't ever see me. Late afternoon when shadows are long I'll look like one more blade of prairie grass. Morning, I'll blend into the river mist. Night, I'll just plain old melt away, not even caught by the silver of a full moon.

May 23, 1804

Today I nearly stepped out of my life as a shadow, though I'm not sure what I could have done to help. Captain Lewis almost got himself killed! Captain Lewis likes to get out of the boat and walk along through the country. He carries a notebook with him and stops and writes and looks at plants and birds. I can't get close enough to see, but I think he draws pictures of some of the things. Today he was hiking through high country that was needled with ragged points that stuck out over the river. He had climbed one and I was way back on lower ground when suddenly I heard him yell. I looked up, and dang if he wasn't hanging off below one of those points, blowing in the breeze like a rag. I started running toward him, but there was no straight line between me and where the Captain hung. Wasn't more than ten minutes had passed when I saw he had done wrenched himself out of this terrible situation and was up on top of the point and walking like nothing had happened. Not even a wobble in his stride. He saved his own hide and I guess I saved my shadow.

May 26, 1804
North side of river, near La Charrette

I was so darn tired tonight that I dumped myself close to camp, though I usually try to sleep a mile or so ahead. There was a good pile of river junk—old uprooted trees, brush, and what-have-you. It makes for a pretty good hide for me. Last night we were in the last settlement, La Charrette, a small French village. I managed to sneak into the village after they had made camp and trade some of my jerky for some headcheese. Then I scuttled through someone's garden at the edge of the village and pulled myself some of their carrots. I know it's stealing. If I were back in St. Charles I'd have to go to confession and tell Father Dumaine. But I just ate the carrots in the moonlight. They tasted so dang good that I can't believe it was a sin. Guess that's how every sinner feels. Mingo probably feels the same way when he drinks whiskey.

Later: Darned if Captain Lewis's dog Seaman didn't discover me in this pile of brush. Two o'clock in the morning and the moon hanging up there like a sliver of a fingernail with clouds scudding over suddenly I felt something warm and wet, kind of rough but nice on my cheek. I thought I was dreaming. Oh! I thought I was being kissed by some beautiful young lady. Then I smelled dog breath. I opened my eyes and if it wasn't that drooling dog of Captain Lewis's, a big old Newfoundland who thought I was just tasty. I'm good with dogs. I didn't startle him or cuss him out or anything. I just scratched his ears. Talked gentle. Actually complimented him for finding me. Then told him to get on his way. He did, real polite-like. Most creatures are polite. You be polite to them, they polite you right back.

June 1, 1804

I'm getting a bit tired of being a shadow. It's getting harder. Drouillard, the Corps' chief scout, and usually two or three men go out every day and hunt. I got to be careful. Drouillard is a crack tracker, so I don't want him fetching up on my prints. Pierre Cruzatte is a good tracker, too. I knew him back in St. Charles. He was a good buddy of François's. They are *voyageurs*, travelers of the river as the French call boatmen. Half-breed, too. Pierre's got one eye. Other one got clawed out by a wildcat. Imagine those two half-breeds Pierre and Francis getting themselves sworn in as honest-to-gosh privates in the United States Army. Other men in the Corps hired along the way before they reached St. Charles were not made privates. The Captain must have thought highly of these two half-breeds. They call Pierre "Pete" for short.

Tell you what else is hard about being a shadow. When

Francis and Pierre and Drouillard bring back meat, as they did last night when they brought down a deer, and once before that a bear, I can smell it cooking. Makes me hungry. On nights when they don't catch meat they just eat hominy and lard. That don't set my mouth juices buzzing none. Those nights are easier. It's lonely, too. Sometimes I can creep up pretty close. I hear them talking, and Francis and Pierre, they sing some French songs they learned at their papas' knees. Guess I was too young when my papa went. Didn't learn any. Got to stop this slobbering here. I ain't no crybaby. Corps of Discovery doesn't want a slobbering fool. Sort of wish Seaman would come visit me tonight. He's done it twice since that first time.

June 2, 1804

We reached the Osage River yesterday. The Captains have ordered men to cut down all the trees so Captain Lewis can make his special observations. He gets out there with some instrument but it ain't a telescope. He peers through it at the sun and then at the moon, too, and then every few minutes he calls, "Mark" and Captain Clark looks at a very large watch. I think I heard them calling it a cro-no-meter. This all has something to do with mapping, but I am not sure what. This is the problem with being a shadow. There is only so much you can learn. Captain Clark is a much better boatman than Captain Lewis. So he is usually on the boat and Lewis just seems to love walking over the land looking at things and drawing.

June 4, 1804

Good hunting. Drouillard and his men are bringing in deer every day. But it doesn't take long for them to be eaten up—not with about forty-five hungry men. Mosquitoes are the devil's own round here. The men got themselves plenty of "voyageurs grease" made from tallow and buffalo fat. I could kick myself for forgetting to bring some of Mingo's. I think I'm providing food for every dang mosquito west of the Mississippi. My ear healed up fine. I don't know what it looks like now, as I haven't a looking glass. Feels kind of nubbly, like it has been chewed on by some critter.

June 6, 1804

I been stretching well out ahead of the Corps and even of Drouillard. I think we're well into Indian country. Found some of their paintings on a big hunk of limestone rock. Just as I'm squatting down studying the marks that they gouged out and painted in with some red and blue paint, I heard a low, fast hiss. By God if I hadn't practically squatted into a nest of rattlesnakes. I ask you, does one Augustus Pelletier have hominy for brains? I should have known better and watched my step. I just about jumped twenty feet straight up into the air.

June 9, 1804
Prairie of Arrows

We're in a stretch of river all cut up with small channels. They call this piece of the country Prairie of Arrows. At one point around here the river narrowed to less than a thousand feet across. Hard navigating. They came close to stoving in the keelboat. Francis and Pierre are their best boatmen, so they watch for whirlpools, snags, and do a lot of the steering. One of them is always at the helm. They met up with some French trappers yesterday, but I met up with them a day earlier. I had two bits in my pocket and done bought me some voyageurs grease off them. It was risky. They might say something about me to the Corps. But I can't stand these mosquitoes another minute. Lot of drifting timber and shoal water in this part of the river. They fetched up on a snag this afternoon, then crossed over to an island to camp tonight. I'm here on the north bank. Glad to be here and not smell their dang meat roasting.

June 12, 1804

More French trappers. Looks to me like they're giving a ride to one of them up the river.

June 13, 1804

I was able to camp real close tonight. Being downwind of them it carried their voices and of course the juicy smells of deer roasting. But I could also hear them. This trapper who they picked up is old Dorion. He used to come through St. Charles all the time. They're taking him back as far as the Sioux nation, the Yankton Sioux who live above the Platte River. His wife is a Yankton, and I guess he's pretty thick with the chiefs. From what I could hear they hope that Dorion can persuade some chiefs to go to Washington to meet President Jefferson.

June 14, 1804

Dang if the ticks, gnats, and mosquitoes aren't unbearable thick out here. They fly up your nose. Can't put the voyageurs grease up my nose else I suffocate. Some choice. Suffocate to death or be bitten to death.

June 17, 1804

Well, this is one night when I am glad I am not a member of the Corps of Discovery. They are all as sick as dogs. Must have had some bad meat or water. They are all out in the bushes with the dysentery. Except for that, the country around here is beautiful. These men puking their guts out don't add to the scenery. Lots of timber on the south side of the river. Lots of elk, deer, bear.

June 20, 1804

I have set myself to studying Captain Lewis. I'm going to learn him like you learn a book. Then one of these days when we're so far out he can't send me back, I'm going to go up and just tell him I want to join and he ain't going to look at me like a little kid hardly no bigger than a feed bag. I began my studies this morning as I shadowed him along the north bank of the river. Within one hour he stopped fifteen times at various plants and opened up his notebook and wrote. He would then either yank up the whole plant or take a sample of several of its leaves, blossoms, or stems, and put them in a bag. He carries another bag for the small game he shoots. I know this game is not for eating—why would he shoot only one grouse that would hardly feed two men when he could have shot a dozen? Nothing escapes this man's eyes. He picks up rocks! I even saw him grab a bug, I think. He had something fluttering between his thumb and first finger that was smaller than a butterfly but bigger than a ladybug.

June 22, 1804

I believe that we are almost four hundred miles up the Missouri River now. My study of Captain Lewis continues. I saw him in camp two nights ago bring out that grouse he'd shot and show it to Captain Clark. I could not hear what they were saying, but Captain Clark went and got paper and drawing materials and set up the bird to make a sketch. So now I know that Clark must draw better than Lewis. I am a pretty fair sketcher myself.

June 23, 1804

Captain Lewis killed two terns today and measured them before putting them in his bag. He has never done this before. I have seen him measure birds he has killed back at the camp. I wonder if he is thinking that something about the bird's size changes a few hours after its death. Maybe it shrinks up or something?

June 24, 1804

Sometimes when I am shadowing Captain Lewis, he seems lost in deep, sad thoughts. Sometimes I think I hear him talking to himself. Captain Lewis does not smile much and he is much quieter than Captain Clark. You can always hear Captain Clark's voice around camp. His laughter laces through the night and dodges the wind. I do not believe I have ever once heard Captain Meriwether Lewis laugh out loud.

June 25, 1804

I stretched on out ahead today. Made good time in spite of the wind. I just sliced across it. The keelboat and the canoes couldn't do that. Anyhow, I done seen the mouth of a new river. I think it's the one they been talking about. The Kansas.

June 27, 1804
At the juncture of the Kansas and Missouri Rivers

Well, this beats all. You ever seen a man weigh water? I did this morning. First Captain Lewis dunked a bucket into the Missouri and weighed it on this scale they haul around. Then he sent someone to fetch a bucket from where the Kansas joins the Missouri and told him to go well downstream. It's one of the privates. I think his name is Reuben, and he came back with it and they weighed it. The Missouri weighs more. I could have told them that. What with the freight of mud and stuff in that water it was bound to weigh more. Captain Clark then went over to the Kansas and measured its breadth. It stands 230 yards wide, compared with the Missouri's 500 yards at this point.

June 29, 1804

It's about two o'clock in the morning, and I don't quite believe what I am seeing. I got a good vantage point from up here on a bluff. Two of the men on guard tonight, two privates, I think their names are John and Hugh, started tapping on the whiskey barrel. Every day the men are allowed one gill of whiskey. I have seen them get it now for the past month. Just one gill. Well, this fellow John comes over and says to Hugh, "Come on, Hugh. No one will notice. We deserve more. Just one!" Just one, my foot! Before you know it, they've gone tapped that barrel a dozen more times, each one. They are getting drunker by the minute.

Later: Dang if they haven't rousted the whole camp with their drunken, loutish talk. The sergeant-at-arms was just called and Captain Clark ordered them put under arrest. I heard him say there would be a trial.

Meanwhile the dawn is coming up all silver and pink. It's a beauty because the sky is perfectly clear and there is a morning moon. I could have told you Captain Lewis wants no part of this trial stuff. He snatched up his notebook and his collecting bag and walked out of camp. I followed him. I just have this sense about things. This feeling. I think this might be my day to join the Corps of Discovery. I think it is time to maybe step out of the shadows and into the light of this morning moon, and show them that I can be a stand-up sort of fellow, a stand-up member of the Corps of Discovery.

June 30, 1804
longitude 94.58 degrees west,
latitude 39.55 degrees north,
Missouri River, north bank

I am a shadow no more. I stepped into the light of this day in front of Captain Meriwether Lewis, first captain of the United States Infantry and commanding captain of the Corps of Discovery, at 8:26 A.M. I know this exact time because, although I do not have a watch, Captain Lewis has three, including the cro-no-meter. Between 7:06 and the time I showed myself, Captain Lewis had measured the distance between the sun and that morning moon forty times. He measured it eight more times.

I would hold the cro-no-meter for him, and when he said, "Mark" I would write down the times. He never even asked who I was until after the eighth time. When I first appeared before him, he did not seem surprised. He just said, "Hold this." Those were the Captain's first words to me. Then he said, "Can you write?" I said yes. He gave me his book and pencils and told me to write down the time as taken from the cro-no-meter when he called "Mark." I now know what he is doing. The instrument he looks through is called a sextant. By fixing the height of a star or the sun or the moon above the horizon and measuring its angle and knowing the exact time, one can figure through mathematics something that is called the longitude and the latitude on earth, anywhere on earth. So through his calculations Captain Lewis, calm as a boiled egg, says we are at 94.58 degrees longitude west and 39.55 degrees latitude north. I think it is the most miraculous thing I have ever seen in my life. To think that numbers can do this! Captain Lewis and I then continued walking through the country, or "naturalizing," as he calls it. I helped him lay out a bird he shot for measuring and wrote the numbers he called out for its wingspan and length in a book, the book he always carries. Then he took me back to camp. It was not perhaps the best of times to arrive, for they were just laying on lashes to the two privates who had been found guilty of drunkenness, fifty lashes to one, and one hundred to the other. But I'm here. You should have seen Francis Labiche and Pierre Cruzatte when I walked into camp. Would have thought they'd seen a ghost. "We're more than two hundred miles from St. Charles!" Francis shouted. "How'd you get here?" "On my own blessed feet," I said. But they both seemed genuinely glad to see me. So I'm here and I ain't no ghost and I ain't no shadow.

July 1, 1804

No ghost has an ear like mine either. That was about the second thing Francis asked me. "Whatcha done to your ear?" I said, "It's more like what Mingo's done. I guess I didn't do the greatest job sewing it up." Francis got hold of a reflecting mirror they use for signaling and I looked at my ear for the first time since I sewed it. It kind of looks like a little piece of dried apple, the kind Mama used to put up for winter sweets. It's all crinkly and a little bit folded over. I decided right then to comb my hair to the other side. Now my hair covers the top, which is the worst part. I'm all right with it. I'm not going to worry about it. Too many good things to think about. Like roasted deer and bear for supper tonight. No more sitting on the edges of juiciness. I'm going to be in there slurping it all up!

July 2, 1804

York, Captain Clark's Negro servant, took me and gave me a new pair of wool pants. I had to chop off the bottoms. They were too long. He let me pick out a blanket, too. Captain Lewis is impressed with my handwriting, and I shall be helping him transcribe information that he is collecting on his "naturalizing" trips, descriptions and measurements of plants and birds and other animals. I am also to take my share of camp chores—cooking, scrubbing. And they will probably set me to guard duty. Both Captains are pleased that I speak some Omaha and French. I know some sign language as well. I was honest with them—told them it is easier for me to understand the sign language than to actually sign. I intend to make myself very useful to both Captains.

July 3, 1804

Many raspberries along the way. I forgot to write that three, four days ago the river changed at a big bend and began heading more northerly than directly west. This eases the glare at the end of the day. But now we talk about the east and the west banks of the river instead of the north and south.

Saw our first sign of beaver today. I told Captain Lewis how tasty beaver steaks are.

July 4, 1804

This is the first Fourth of July celebration west of the Mississippi. The men fired a cannon at dawn today. Fired it west to let the world know we're coming! It was pretty exciting to be part of this. I had it in my mind that beaver might taste good, this being a holiday and all. The men are pretty tired of deer meat. So the Captains said Reuben Field and his brother Joseph, who have been quite friendly to me and are very cheerful sorts, could go ahead on foot and scout for beaver along the banks. All of a sudden I heard a yelp from the direction that Joe Field had gone. Quick as a greased bolt I ran up a path and there he was, crumpled down in the dust holding his hand. He'd reached down to pick a blackberry and a rattler done picked him. I could see the two ugly little black dots just round and perfect as anything where the snake's fangs punctured him. I made the x's and sucked real hard. Reuben Field came up and immediately saw what had happened.

It was near noon, and the keelboat and canoes had pulled ashore at the start of a creek. So we got him down there and Captain Lewis got out his medical kit that Dr. Rush from Philadelphia outfitted him with. I'd never heard of Dr. Rush, but I guess he is the most famous doctoring man in the Union. He makes these famous pills called Dr. Rush's Thunderclappers that blast you out if your bowels get gummed up and stuck. But that ain't what Captain Lewis used on Joe Field. He first mashed up shreds of some kind of tree bark and mixed it with a strong minty-smelling ointment. It seemed to work. His hand hardly swelled up at all.

To me the most exciting part of the day was not the cannon, which they blasted twice, or poor Joe Field getting bit by the rattler, but the naming of the creek where we stopped at midday. The Captains named it Independence Creek. I never before thought about naming things like this. I know my mama and I named that island back near St. Charles, but it was just like our own private name. Here the Captains name things not just for private. They mark it down on the map Captain Clark is making for the expedition. Everybody in the whole country will know that the name of this creek is Independence and that the Corps of Discovery has named it. There is something mighty exciting about being part of a group that names things. We are truthfully naming America! That is a powerful notion.

July 5, 1804

Something special happened today. Captain Lewis showed me the letter from President Jefferson to him, giving the instructions for the expedition. I asked if I could copy a part of it down. Here it is:

To Meriwether Lewis, esquire, Captain of the 1st regiment of infantry of the United States of America:

The object of your mission is to explore the Missouri river, & such principal stream of it, as, by its course and communication with the waters of the Pacific Ocean, may offer the most direct & practicable water communication across this continent, for the purposes of commerce.

Jefferson

Pr. U.S. of America

I already knew that the purpose of the expedition was to explore beyond the Missouri and all this new land that came with the Louisiana Purchase, but I wasn't clear on the fact that the real dream, the big hope, is an all-water route to the Pacific.

The most exciting thing to me is that I have actually touched a paper touched by President Jefferson, and here I am just a poor half-breed boy. But brother, am I glad my mama done sent me to Father Dumaine back when I was little to learn how to read and write. The paper wouldn't have meant half so much if I hadn't been able to read it.

July 8, 1804

Dang! If I wasn't right. We saw Indian fires on the east bank of the river tonight. Nothing's come of it so far. But we all stand guard in shorter shifts with more men. The Captains want us on the alert and not too tired.

July 10, 1804

I got us a beaver today. Then Drouillard got another two. So there was just about enough to go around. Captain Clark joked that now I've done spoiled the men's taste for "portable soup." All the men groaned. I haven't had it yet. It's not something that you want to eat. They only had it when they had a dry spell in hunting a month or so back. The soup is thick as frozen bear lard and is made from boiling beef jerky, eggs, and root vegetables. Captain Clark is a fair jokey fellow. He's always smiling and you can even see it behind that big brush of a red beard. Captain Lewis never jokes. But I don't mind his quiet. Sometimes I go into his tent to help with the journalizing—that's what he calls this note keeping on the plants and animals. In the yellow light of the burning candle he casts a hunched shadow against the canvas sides of the tent. I can tell just by the hunchiness how he's feeling. Sometimes he doesn't say a word and just slides the field notes toward me to recopy. Tonight he said exactly three words to me. "Nice mud trout." I had done a drawing of these speckled fish we call the mud trout, which we see a lot of. Some folks wouldn't be satisfied with just three words, but I'm fine with it.

July 11, 1804

Drouillard, who scouts out way ahead, came back this evening and reckons that we are no more than seventy-five miles short of the Platte River. I have never known any man, French trapper, or Missouri boatman who has gone beyond the Platte. I can hardly believe I will. A year ago if someone had told me I'd be going beyond the Platte, well, they might as well have told me I was going to the moon.

July 13, 1804

Private Willard fell asleep on guard duty last night. It was Sergeant Ordway who found him. Charged him of being "guilty of lying down and sleeping on his post." Willard, who I've got to say has pluck, replied, "Guilty of lying down and not guilty of going to sleep." Nonetheless it earned him one hundred lashes every day for four days, beginning at sunset.

July 14, 1804

Hard driving rains since dawn. Then all of a sudden the sky turned black and a wind drove down on us from the northeast. I was riding in the big keelboat. It hit on the starboard side, the right side, just as we were passing a sand island. We would have been dashed to bits in one minute, but we all leaped to the downwind side of the boat and threw over an anchor and cable lines. Canoes were in the same fix. We did ship some water. Storm kept barreling down on us for half an hour or more.

July 15, 1804

Captain Clark set York and me to the task of checking equipment and provisions, in particular the gifts for the Indians, to see if they were hurt by all the water we shipped. Even though there were tarpaulins covering most everything, some of the tarps have big tears in them. York is a good fellow. He's jokey like his master. They fit well together. Anyhow we spread all sorts of gear out on the beach. I can't hardly believe how much trading material they have for the Indians. There's five pounds of white glass beads, and that's just the white ones, twenty pounds of red, and at least twenty-five pounds of blue, because Captain Lewis has this notion that the Indians like blue beads the best. There's exactly 288 thimbles. I had to count them and ten pounds of sewing thread, a whole mess of combs, and armbands and ear trinkets.

Now, that's just the gifts for the Indians. Then there's Dr. Rush's medical kit with all manner of vials and little jars stuffed with pills or ointments and bandages. There are Kentucky rifles. I ain't never seen anything as beautiful as these muzzle-loading, flintlock, and long-barreled rifles. Everyone calls them Kentucky rifles but their real name is U.S. Model 1803. Joe Field told me they are the first rifle specifically designed for the United States Army. Captain Lewis made the redesign. It took us all morning to check everything over. Nothing was too wet. Maybe lost a five-pound bag of flour, that's all.

July 16, 1804

Some men are part of the permanent party, which means that they will go all the way to the Shining Sea, while others will head back to St. Louis after we winter over somewhere in Mandan country. I didn't know until a few days ago that not everyone was going to make the whole trip. This business about a "permanent party" and whatever they call the others — I call them the turnarounds — has got me more than a mite scared. I sure thought I was most certainly going all the way to the Pacific Ocean. I have no idea where I stand and I'm scared to ask Captain Lewis. I'm just going to keep trying as hard as I can to copy his notes. And I'm getting real good with the sextant and the quadrant—lining up stars over the horizon. I hope they decide I'm worth it and will take me all the way. There's a word in Omaha for what I want to be. It's hard to explain but it means roughly good-thing-held-tight-in-the-fist. My mama used to say this word when we got a big catfish out of the river that gleamed with a bright eye. They were the best. I think I'm one of these. I think I'm a keeper.

July 19, 1804

I like Joe and Reuben Field a lot. They are real nice to me. Joe surely appreciates that I carved into his hand with my knife and sucked out the snake venom. He says that saved him as much as Dr. Rush's poultice that the Captain slapped on him. He and Reuben were personally selected by Captain Clark at the very start. They come from his country—Kentucky—and were known to be the best woodsmen and hunters around. They could almost be twins. Joe's face is a little leaner than Reuben's and I think he's a tad taller, but their voices and their laugh is just the same. If I've got my back turned and one of them comes up and says, "Hey, Gus," I don't know which one it is until I turn around. Must be something great having a brother and being on an expedition like this. In the hugeness of this land—it is getting huger every day as it flattens out into the plains ahead—it must feel good to have kin within spitting distance.

July 22, 1804

Reached the mouth of the Platte yesterday. Captain Lewis has kept me busy enough for three men. When he gets to a geography—be it a river coming in, a creek, or a stretch of land that changes from prairie to plains—the man just about goes crazy with his note taking and scientific measurements. Water, I think, is Captain Lewis's favorite thing to weigh, to measure, and to cogitate about. He's gone plumb crazy with this Platte, which in my considered opinion is a lousy excuse for a river. It is great and wide but it slides along barely an inch deep in some places. The thing that Captain Lewis keeps going on about is how much sand there is in this river. Well, I guess if you like rivers made from sand you would fancy this one. I personally prefer water in my rivers. The river is cut by about a thousand channels, some as skinny as a starved mule. We had to count a mess of these and measure their width. Then he had me help him make a million measurements on the velocity of the river—that means the speed. We dropped in things like feathers and then timed them with the cro-no-meter. Then he tasted it to see if it was salty. There is not a thing that man has not done to that poor bedraggled river. And if that was not enough he went off and started measuring some of the grass along the banks. I, of course, had to help transcribe all these notes this evening. I better quit now and turn in. My hands are like to cramp up from all the writing.

July 23, 1804

We are camped above a small willow island. Lots of timber around—oak, elm, walnut. The Captains want to stay here for a few days since it's such a nice spot. We're really near Indians, and the Captains hope to meet some of the chiefs. They sent me out with York and the Field brothers to look for good timber for making oars. They need some spares for the keelboat.

July 25, 1804

We saw an interesting thing today. It was a pointy-top boulder standing twenty feet high and was capped off with a big buffalo skull. Seems to say plain as day that there are Indians around here. I know I've said that before, but a big old buffalo skull doesn't just move up and put itself on top of a rock like that.

July 26, 1804

I like all the men in this outfit but one of them troubles me some. His name is Moses Reed. Whenever he's got some drudge work job that no one might want, he turns to me. I can rightfully say that he is the only one on this expedition who does not treat me like a stand-up member. He seems to think that because I'm the youngest and scrawny, I can be bossed around. Sometimes he treats York this way, too, but never in front of Captain Clark, because he knows Captain Clark won't tolerate anyone treating York like some field hand. Francis came up to him once when Reed was asking me to cut his share of firewood for the cook fires and said, "Just because Gus is on firewood with you today doesn't mean he has to cut your share, Reed!" He glared at him. There's a way a grown-up half-breed, 'specially with French blood, can glare, where their brow turns dark just like storm clouds rolling up on the horizon. I'm working on it myself. It's best with whiskers. I don't have whiskers yet.

July 27, 1804

I caught three dozen catfish for dinner tonight. Nearly one per man. And they're fat, too!

July 28, 1804
Sioux Indian country

First Indian! He was brought in by Drouillard, who'd gone off to hunt. He's a Missouri Indian who lives with ones he calls the Otoes, and he told Drouillard and Francis and Pierre, through sign language, that their camp is about four miles from here but that everyone has gone off to hunt buffalo excepting for him and a few others. Well, finally, an Indian! And that explains why Drouillard and Pierre a few days ago kept finding signs and even one empty Ottawa village. The Captains sent out this Indian with a message to deliver to the others, saying that we want to meet with them.

July 29, 1804

Can't believe it! Reed tried to push off water hauling on me today. But Charley Floyd, he's a quiet kind of fellow, a sergeant in the permanent party, he come up and said real quiet but steady as a rock, "Don't you go asking Gus to do what ain't his job. It's not right, Moses."

July 30, 1804

I was on my way to catch up with Captains Lewis and Clark because they were both out naturalizing and sent for me and more paper and scientific equipment. Well, about a quarter mile before I got to where they was, I came upon this pond and I had to blink. I thought, Dang! Is this thing filled with ice floes in the middle of summer? It wasn't ice. It was a huge flock of swans. Found Lewis and Clark on a bluff. Clark was his usual self, exclaiming, shouting about the beauty of the country that stretched out before them, and Lewis— Lewis was quiet as could be, looking straight down at some bug crawling over his boot. I think in a funny way they are the perfect fit. It is as if Captain Clark can see all the way to the Shining Sea. He sees the contours and the shape of the bones of the land, but it is Lewis who sees every little grain and clod and can measure the pulse and the beat of every heart, whether it be in a mouse or an eagle or a badger.

Later: Badger! Funny I should write that word. Joe Field just came in with one he shot, and Captain Lewis has decided he wants to gut it and stuff it and send it back as a present to President Jefferson. I helped him weigh it and measure it, even its teeth, for Lord's sake. It was kind of interesting watching him gut it and stuff it with a bunch of wadding that had been soaked in preservatives. Captain Lewis thinks this badger is just great, and he had me write, "This is a singular animal not common to any part of the United States." I didn't want to correct him, 'specially seeing as he is sending this one as a present to Jefferson, but I've seen passels of badgers. I like this stuffing dead animals. He calls it "taxidermy." The real fun is that when you've got them almost stuffed you try to set them up in a pose that looks like the way they might have been in life. I wanted to have the badger's left paw raised just a bit as if it were clawing at something, but it kept tipping over. A while back I helped him stuff a rat. I guess it was a special kind of rat, rare and "unique," at least that's what he said. A rat's a rat as far as I can see.

August 1, 1804

Two of the scouting horses wandered off last night. The Captains are worried that the Indian didn't deliver our message, for no Indians have come to meet us.

Sergeant Floyd and I went out to scout the nearby countryside. I spotted a bird that I knew Captain Lewis would want a specimen of. I thought I had him in my sights but missed. But by gosh if Sergeant Floyd didn't get him two seconds later. Floyd is one powerful shot to bring down a spooked bird after it had been missed once. I said to him, "Thanks, Sergeant Floyd." And he said to me, "Just call me Charley, Gus." Then I said, "You sure are a fine shot, Charley," and you know what he said to me? He said, "I wish I could draw that bird half as fine as you're going to draw it." I couldn't believe that he had seen my drawings. He said that Captain Lewis showed him some.

It's Captain Clark's thirty-fourth birthday today. I had no idea he was so old. We celebrated with the tastiest dinner so far. A saddle of venison, beaver tail steaks, elk, and a dessert that York made of cherries, plums, raspberries, and currants.

August 2, 1804

Horses found. Private John Colter and Drouillard brought them back into camp this morning along with elk they shot. Finally some of the Otoes and Missouri nation came to camp with a trader who lives among them. Wouldn't you know they'd show when Captain Lewis had sent me back out with his dang specimen bag to collect some weeds he's taken a fancy to. They traded some roasted meat and flour to the Indians for some watermelons.

August 3, 1804

Indians came back today with more from their village including six chiefs, but not the top one. York and I set up the mainsail of the keelboat as an awning. They met under it. Captain Lewis made what I call the Big Speech. He done told me about it several times. In fact I had to copy it out three times. He don't want to lose it, and I heard him practice it with Pierre and Francis and Drouillard because they have to put it in sign language. In it he tells them why we are here, where we are going, and that they have a new Great Father—Jefferson. The first two parts of the speech I kept thinking would go over fine. But I couldn't help but wonder if these Indians would be a little bit surprised to hear they have a new Great White Father back in Washington. He also calls them "children." Maybe that doesn't strike others wrongly, but me being the youngest I think it's odd calling these grown men "children," especially the chiefs. The Indians, however, seemed fine with this information. Didn't twitch an eyebrow. We gave them gunpowder and a bottle of whiskey to share around. Then we gave each of the six chiefs a special medal to hang around his neck. I was sent to fetch some paint and dress ornaments but told to leave back the blue bead bags. Captain Lewis told me we have to make them last all the way to the Shining Sea. Of course I think we've got enough to last all the way across the whole dang sea. Hard to imagine using up twenty-five pounds of blue beads.

We named this meeting place Council Bluffs. Makes sense, I guess, for this is the first place we took council with the Indians.

August 4, 1804

Well, it looks like Moses Reed has up and deserted. Yesterday after the council with the Indians we made our way upstream and camped on a sandy point on the western side of the river. Reed told me to tell the Captains that he had left his knife back at the other campsite at Council Bluffs and was going back to fetch it. He ain't been heard from since.

Later: Still no sign of Reed.

August 5, 1804

Captain Lewis is busy killing animals for study. I am kept equally busy helping him measure and weigh. Now he asks me to draw more often. We got a bull snake today and two water birds, one that squeaked like a pig— honest to gosh. I had to write that in the notebook, but it's true. We crouched and listened to it squeaking away for a good five minutes before Captain shot it.

York asked me to help him mend some tarp today but Captain Lewis needed me. Pierre Cruzatte came up and said, "York, you don't want this boy mending tarp. Look how he done sewed his ear." York and I laughed. As a matter of fact, I've become a better sewer helping Captain Lewis stuff all these critters. You have to sew up the seams.

August 7, 1804

I don't think there is a night I go to sleep not thinking about whether I am going to be able to be a member of the permanent party and go all the way to the Shining Sea. But I can't get up my nerve to ask Captain Lewis. I have been thinking that I've got to talk to someone about this and the person I might best be able to confide in is either York or Charley Floyd. York might be a Negro and a slave, but he is a stand-up man in my book, as is Charley.

August 8, 1804

This morning we had a good southeasterly breeze. Doesn't often happen and we could hoist the sail on the keelboat. I was riding lookout up front, although lately I've been doing my share of pulling and poling—poling off sandbars. Anyhow we come round the bend and it looks like the whole river had been covered with a white blanket. First, I thought, Swans, like back before at that pond. But then I see that these ain't no swans. Captain Lewis was about to jump out of his skin. He's leaning so far out with his seeing scope that Joe Field has to hold on to him by the pants so he won't fall into the river. Then he yelps "Birds of Clime! Birds of Clime!" and before I know it he has us pull over and Captain Lewis, Joe and Reuben Field, Drouillard, and I are out of the boat.

Drouillard is the party's best shot, but Joe and Reuben aren't bad. The Captain and I are the only ones without rifles. We're carrying all the scientific equipment to note take and measure. Captain shoves a field notebook into my hands and starts dictating facts to me as we walk. I'm getting expert at walking and listening and writing all at the same time. No neat trick. Anyhow, Captain is going on and on, he's so excited. I guess these birds—he calls them pelicans—spend the winter on the coast of Florida—I am not sure where Florida is—and then go over to the Gulf of Mexico. Not sure where that gulf is either. Captain Lewis knows all this from book learning, and he is sure these are the white pelicans he has read about.

August 13, 1804

Set up camp on a sand island today. Pierre Cruzatte along with a few others was sent to take a message to the Omaha Indian village, inviting them back to our camp tomorrow. Yesterday we saw a strange animal. Looked like a cross between a dog and a fox to me, but Captain Lewis called it a prairie wolf. They tried to kill one to stuff but it got away. Looks pretty fast and sneaky to me. Charley Floyd should have been here. He would have got him, but Charley was feeling poorly this morning.

August 17, 1804

I brought Charley some bread and coffee for breakfast this morning. He is still feeling sick. He couldn't touch it. Said it would make him sicker.

Francis has been out scouting with Drouillard these several days. He came back into camp tonight and says Drouillard is following with Reed and three Oto chiefs. They done found him. There will be a court-martial as soon as they come back.

August 18, 1804

Got to hand it to Reed. He confessed everything, even stealing a rifle, and was as stand-up as I'd seen him since I've known him. Didn't flinch and try to dodge out of anything. Think it impressed the Captains. At least they didn't order him shot. They could have. Instead they ordered him to run the gauntlet four times through the entire party, and they gave each one a switch, and we were every one of us ordered to whip him as he came through. That means in all over 100 lashes. I must say that I didn't have much stomach for it even though I don't like the fellow. But I did it. The chiefs were shocked by this punishment but the Captains explained its rightfulness. It's Captain Lewis's thirtieth birthday today, and because of it they passed out extra gills of whiskey. Took a tiny sip.

Didn't like it. Seemed to sting as much as a whipping would. Me and Charley were the only ones who didn't drink. The calomel doses Captain Lewis gives Charley don't seem to help much.

August 19, 1804

Imagine this: I wake up this morning. Just going out to take a leak when I look up and dang if I don't see a half-naked Indian coming into camp. And a chief he turns out to be! Came to show how poor he was. His name is Big Horse. The Captains invited him to stay for breakfast under the awning, and Captain Lewis asked that I come to take some notes. I have never eaten breakfast with a naked person before.

August 20, 1804

I heard a stirring and a lot of voices, including Captain Lewis's, right before dawn. I could tell something not good was happening. There was this strange hush and just something about the way the Captains were standing when I came to see what was taking place. What I found was that Sergeant Floyd was dying. Just as the sun broke over the horizon he breathed his last.

Sergeant Charles Floyd is the first U.S. soldier to die

west of the Mississippi. We buried him this afternoon on a bluff overlooking a river. Captain Lewis read the funeral service, and Captain Clark called him "a man who at all times gave proofs of his firmness and determined resolution to do service to his country and honor himself." The best part of the service was at the end when the Captains officially named the little river Floyd's River and the bluff Sergeant Floyd's Bluff. Here we are, naming America again, and you couldn't have a better name than Floyd to pin onto a bluff, a river, or a creek. Charley Floyd was a stand-up man.

August 21, 1804

I can't stop thinking about Charley. I really miss him. When I'm riding up front on the keelboat I catch myself just staring down at the water as it slides under us, and I keep thinking every foot up this river we're farther and farther from Charley, and I think it seems so lonely—him buried out on that high bluff. Then I get all morbid and think about his body under that red cedar post we made to mark his grave. I think about it rotting away and turning to dust and sinking down into the earth and maybe spilling down that hill with the first good rains when they wash out dirt. Then I think about it going into the river—maybe not this big one but the little one, Floyd's

River, and all that dust that was Charley just mixes with the silt and the water of the river and then . . . and I guess it just floats away.

August 22, 1804

Good mileage last two days. About forty. This evening we held an election to vote for Charley's replacement in the permanent party. Privates Patrick Gass and William Bratton and George Gibson were nominated. Not me! But I can't complain. I was allowed to vote. I couldn't believe it. So was York. And I figure this is the first election ever held west of the Mississippi. I liked voting. It felt like a real stand-up thing to do. I voted for Gass. And he won.

August 23, 1804

Joe Field came running back into camp hollering his dang head off. He'd done killed a buffalo! I guess we couldn't have any surer sign that we are on the great plains than a buffalo. Captain Lewis took eight men out with him, me included. We brought horses to drag the buffalo into the boat. I never seen anything so huge. We roasted the hump and the tongue that night and cut the rest up into steaks. I tell you, buffalo is nearly as good as beaver in my book. My mouth still waters just from the memory.

August 26, 1804

Private Shannon is missing. Everyone seems pretty sure he has not deserted. We think he's just plain lost. The Captains sent Colter out to look for him.

August 27, 1804

Still no sign of Shannon. The Captains now have sent out Drouillard. We are approaching Yankton Sioux country. This is the home ground for the French trader who has been along with us, Old Dorion. President Jefferson asked Captain Lewis to council with all the Plains nations, but with the Sioux in particular. We set a prairie fire to warn the Indians that we are coming. It's going to be time for Dorion to earn his keep, says Reuben Field. He hasn't done a lick of work, and he ate more buffalo hump than anybody the other night. So he better start translating real good and I hope his wife's as tight with the chiefs as he says she is.

August 28, 1804

Dorion got the Indians here all right, seventy of them and the five chiefs. They came whooping and hollering into camp with their drums, blowing on their pipes, and all painted up. We had a council with them at the bluffs.

Captain Lewis made the Big Speech. I got the scissors, some iron pots, tobacco and corn, and the beads (not too many blue, as Captain Lewis warned me). I am already tired of this speech. I wish I could have gone with Sergeant Pryor the day before. He got to go into the Yankton village. He came back with wonderful tales. He says these Indians live in cone-shaped tents made from buffalo hide that they paint bright colored designs on. I can't imagine such tents. And do you know what they fed him for dinner? Roasted dog. He said it was tasty. I told Captain Lewis we better keep a sharp eye on Seaman. We sure don't want him ending up on a spit.

These Plains Indians paint themselves up all gaudy and decorate their clothes with porcupine quills and feathers. Captain Lewis called me into his tent after they left and he wrote, then dictated to me a long piece on how they dressed.

August 31, 1804

Another meeting this morning with the chiefs. They say that despite these fancy clothes they are really poor. Their women have no clothes. This is just their fancy dress-up duds for dancing and meeting other chiefs. They want whiskey and they want guns and gunpowder, but the last chief who spoke, Arcawechar, warned the Captains that

the Corps is going to need all its powder as it goes farther west.

September 7, 1804

We're in the short-grass country now. Saw the strang-
est little critters. Yesterday I was walking out with the
Captain not far from the campsite when all of a sudden
we heard these high little squeaks, sounded like pip . . .
pip . . . pip. Then we saw these tiny heads poke out of
dirt mounds. Their heads look a little like squirrels but
not the rest of them. Dorion told us they call them *petit
chiens*—little dogs. We just started calling them prairie dogs or barking squirrels. They live underground and
have built a whole mess of connecting tunnels. Clever
little fellows!

September 8, 1804

Dang if Captain Lewis didn't bring five of us out to dig
into these underground prairie dog villages, and dang if
they aren't deeper than anyone thought. There is no getting to the bottom here, and I surely hope the Captain
gives up this idea fast.

Later: The Captain's new idea is to flush them out. We
had to lug five barrels of water out here and pour it into a

hole. Sure enough, the animals started to come out. The Captain ordered us to capture one live. He wants to send it back to President Jefferson. So we did. And who's in charge of taking care of it? Me.

September 9, 1804

When I got a close look at this barking squirrel we done captured, I thought, By jig if this critter ain't the spitting image of Brother Antoine. Brother Antoine, or Frère Antoine, as he was known in St. Charles, was a Jesuit monk who came out to help Father Dumaine a couple of years ago. He was kind of a squirrely little guy. So I named this critter here Antoine.

September 11, 1804

Shannon was found today. We spotted him sitting on the bank just as the keelboat made a bend in the river. He has near starved to death. The fellow must be dumb as a stump. This is God's country out here. He could have fished. Killed himself a deer. Next to me Shannon is the youngest on the expedition. He's almost twenty. That's six years older than me.

September 17, 1804

I saw something today that my eyes still do not believe. We were on a high bluff—the Captains, Drouillard, and the Field brothers—and we looked down and saw a blanket of blackness stretched as far as we could see over the plains. You could see slow waves in it and a roiling motion as it drew closer. It was a herd of thousands of buffalo. It was a most amazing sight. This whole country is filled with game. Every place you look are elk, deer, wild turkeys, and pronghorn goats. The pronghorns are the fastest critters on four feet I have ever seen. They are real hard to get a shot at. Captain Lewis has tried and always misses.

September 23, 1804

Fair breezes from the east. We are able to hoist the mainsail and make good time. I am becoming one of the best at hoisting the sails. You have to do it quick or it can get caught midway up the pole. Then they ask me to scramble up there because I am light and can slide out the crosspiece easy. There is a kind of nervousness in the air, however, despite the fair winds. Everyone is worried about the Teton Sioux. They are much different and less peaceable than the Yankton Sioux. The Captains are short with the men for the first time ever. Even Captain Clark, usually so even-tempered, looks like he is a fuse already burning with that red beard. Pierre speaks some of this kind of Sioux language.

September 25, 1804

Three chiefs came to camp today. They brought them out onto the keelboat for the meeting. There were many warriors with them who stayed on shore. They brought buffalo meat as a gift. Pierre was no good at the translating. He only knew a few words and I guess not the right ones. Beforehand I was sent for the beads—lots of blue ones this time! And I was told to bring back a magnifying glass as well. We even brought out the air gun, corn, tobacco, and whiskey. The medals were given as the last part of the gift giving. And then there was this god-awful silence and the chiefs just stared. It was as if we had all fallen into a deep, dark hole. I knew something had gone terribly wrong. Then one of the chiefs, the one called Buffalo Medicine, signed. No interpreting was needed. The sign was clear as anything: "Is this all?" You knew that the chief thought these were stupid gifts and that he didn't give a hoot what colored beads we gave them and that they thought the medals with the profile of Jefferson were about as precious as horse dung.

More whiskey was offered and then the trouble began. The chief made ugly, rude signs right to Captain Clark. No interpreter needed. They were not going to leave when the canoes were brought up to fetch them to go ashore. Captain Clark really had to force them into the canoes. Then when the canoes landed, two or three warriors caught hold of the bow lines and wouldn't let go. They started yammering. I guess it was about the presents and how they weren't any good. Captain Clark grew red all over. I swear even his hands looked bright when he drew his sword. I could see from where I was on the keelboat. Then I felt the keelboat rock as Captain Lewis swiveled the cannon on the bow and pointed it right toward the warriors on shore. He stood there with a lit taper over the cannon. There were sixteen musket balls ready to tear loose down the throat of that thing, and there were at least seventy warriors on shore who were notching their arrows. You might think that the Indians weren't a fair match for us. But they were, even without a cannon, because they could reload a lot faster than we could. The entire expedition could have ended right then and there. Lewis and Clark could have been killed, along with a passel of the rest of us. It was a moment that seemed to last forever. I kept waiting for one of the Captains to cry, "Fire," but then Buffalo Medicine somehow changed his mind and ordered his men to leave. It could have so easily gone the other way. It would have been awfully simple for the Captains to say the single word "Fire," but something made them delay maybe just three seconds, and that made all the difference.

I might have learned the most important lesson of my life so far today. Sometimes it pays to wait even if it is only three seconds.

Later

I guess one of the things that made the chiefs back off is that the one called Black Buffalo demanded that we come to his village so his wives and children could see the party, especially York. All the Indians we've met so far can't quite believe that York is real. They ain't never seen a black man before. So we went. Black Buffalo was on his best behavior. Couldn't be polite enough. They smoked the peace pipe together and then—I guess they thought this was a big treat—they invited us to watch the Scalp Dance. All the women formed a solid block and began jiggling a pole rattling with deer hooves, but when I looked a little closer, I saw some of those poles had hair attached. Dang if they hadn't strung up the scalps of some Indians they had just led a raid on. I like to died when Francis leaned over and said to me that those scalps belonged to Omaha. Francis and Pierre and I are Omaha! Lordy, I'm glad my father married my mother and brought her in from the plains to St. Charles. I mean, her dying was bad enough. She had pneumonia and her lungs done clogged up and I'll never forget that awful breathing, but the good Lord let her keep her scalp attached to her head at least.

October 5, 1804

Most of the Teton Sioux are well behind us. We were nervous right up to the end. Cruzatte had heard a lot of rumors through the Omaha prisoners they hadn't scalped that the Tetons planned to rob us right before we left. But it was only a rumor, I guess, because it never came to be. We did, however, name one small river that runs into the Missouri the Bad Teton River!

The days are clear and bright. The wind backed round to south the other day and we made more than twenty miles under our sail alone! Each day the shadows grow longer. I like in particular the end of the days, those short late afternoons when the sun drops down and turns everything to gold. We see vast herds of elk and pronghorn coming down to graze in the grassy flats. Captain Lewis seems perkier. I didn't mention it but he was real down through most of last month and hardly ever wrote in his journal. I had to do most of the journalizing. Now he's writing again, but mostly he's out every day walking and collecting. He complimented me on my handwriting today. I seem to be pleasing him. Yet I still don't know if this means that I shall remain as a member of the permanent party. I have decided not to ask York about it. I think I'll just wait and see what happens.

October 7, 1804

I've been forgetting to write about Antoine our prairie dog. He is a frisky little fellow. Doesn't seem to mind not being underground that much. Captain Lewis was worried about that. He's getting right plump. He is the only member of the Corps of Discovery that actually likes the portable soup! I don't even boil it up for him or add water or anything. He just takes it out of the keg in hunks.

October 8, 1804

We're nearing the country of the Arikara Indians. We began seeing signs of their villages a couple of days ago but they seemed abandoned. We couldn't figure this out. Then we came to one in the middle of an island in the river today that had people. We began seeing some of these villagers yesterday in their bull boats, which look like huge bowls floating down the river. They are made from a willow frame with a single buffalo hide stretched over them, and they hold as many as eight people!

October 9, 1804

Moses Reed was actually nice to me today. Offered to help me haul some water. Maybe I'm wrong to say this, but it makes me nervous when someone as naturally ornery and cantankerous as Reed turns all of a sudden nice.

October 10, 1804

Reed came looking for me today. He offered to help me chop firewood. So I said fine, and as we're splitting the wood he starts saying ugly things about the Captains. I just closed my ears. I don't know what's wrong with him. But as I have said before, he ain't no stand-up fellow. So it pays to be watchful.

October 11, 1804

Time for the Big Speech again. The medals, the beads, thread, tobacco, but no whiskey. These Indians didn't seem to care for it or for things at all. The thing they liked most was York. Especially the women!! His complexion is a mystery to them. York was real nice to everyone. He played games with the children. Chased them about, laughing. Everyone came up to touch him. They thought he was "big medicine," as they say, meaning he has a powerful spirit. I guess they need big medicine, as they told us through sign language that the smallpox had swept through these parts about two or three years ago.

Their houses look like the same shape as their boats— round like upside-down bowls. They are made of earth—earth lodges, the Captains call them.

October 13, 1804

Moses Reed is in trouble again. I figured something was going on, with him being so nice to me. He was trying to start what they call a mutiny, a war against the Captains. That's why he had been saying those nasty things about them to me. I guess Private John Newman listened to him and maybe felt the same way. Newman started shouting down Captain Clark at the noonday meal. Before you know it both Reed and Newman were arrested and court-martialed. They both got a sentence of seventy-five lashes. Reed was already stripped of his rank, but now they busted Newman and took him off the permanent party. I feel bad that Newman was so dumb to wind up with a bleeding back and kicked off the permanent party, but maybe they'll need a replacement.

October 16, 1804

Every day we see flocks of geese heading south. Last night there was a good frost. Captain Clark is having trouble with his rheumatism. Captain Lewis treats this by heating up a large stone and wrapping it in flannel. Clark is supposed to sleep with it at night.

October 23, 1804

Captain Lewis has stopped writing again. I think he is feeling very poorly in spirits. My guess is that he realizes that we are not going to reach the headwaters of the Missouri by winter as he had hoped. We're getting to Mandan country now. We'll have to camp around here soon for winter. They say there are some mountains about the size of the ones in Virginia. They expect the headwaters to be at the eastern base of these mountains. They talk about a day or two trip over these mountains and then another river that spills down into the western sea. This river is longer than anyone ever thought. I don't know what to say to Captain Lewis but he's in really bad shape over this. But what can you say about a river that seems to go on forever? I try to imagine its end but I can't.

October 24, 1804
Mandan country

Saw our first Mandans today. The French trader Joseph Gravelines, who helped us some with interpreting with the Arikara, is still with us, and he introduced Captain Lewis to Chief Big White. Captain Lewis went off to their village, and when he came back he reported that they were very friendly. One thing the Captains want to do is help make peace between the Mandans and the Arikara, who have been enemies. He thinks this is possible. So Captain Lewis seems a lot better tonight. Part of Jefferson's instructions, in addition to finding the all-water route, is for all the tribes of the land to live in peace. Captain Lewis is always happy when he can do something for the President, whether it's sending back fat little Antoine or making peace with the Indians.

October 25, 1804

Saw a weasel early this morning. Its fur had turned nearly all white. Sure sign winter is coming.

November 1, 1804

There are two big Mandan villages. The one on the west bank is led by Chief Big White and one farther up on the east bank is led by Black Cat. Then not far away there are three Hidatsa villages led by a chief called Black Moccasin and another by a chief that everyone says is a nasty son of a gun the interpreter calls One Eyed Man, because that's all he's got. The Hidatsa are part of a larger tribe called the Minnetaree people. The Captains had a meeting with us this morning and told us how they plan to build a fort here for us to winter over in. It will be about seven miles below the river the Mandans call the Knife and just across from the lower Mandan village.

November 4, 1804

Work began today on the fort. Everyone works hard. Patrick Gass is the main carpenter. He's dang good. He can make a tight joint. I'd like him to teach me how to make a dovetail joint. We are building two rows of huts, then a big high fence of stakes, a gate and a sentry post, and a big block for mounting the swivel cannon. I don't mind the work even though it's cold and the snow flurries have been swirling down on us all day. The Mandans seem real friendly and come over from their village to watch. Mostly they watch York, but a little boy not more than eight or nine started helping me carry split logs for the huts. He was a nice little fellow so I took him over and introduced him to Antoine, which made him very happy. Pretty soon I had every kid in the village coming up wanting to meet Antoine. I should have charged admission. I'd be a rich man.

November 5, 1804

A French trapper by the name of Toussaint Charbonneau has been around. I heard him speaking French with Pierre and Francis. He's a braggart. In any case, he must have impressed the Captains 'cause he's coming along with us when we break camp in the spring to help with translating.

November 6, 1804

I was standing guard last night. It was freezing cold and I was stomping around, slapping my arms against my sides to keep the blood moving, when I noticed this odd change of light in the darkness. I looked up and it was as if curtains of green and gold and blue were moving across the sky. I'd never seen such a thing. The colors waved as if they were blown by the breath of God, and the stars shined through these curtains. I ran to rouse the rest of the camp and they all came and watched. Captain Lewis calls these the northern lights.

Then I remembered that I had heard tell of them from Mama. She had seen them when she was a little girl out on the plains. She said that they were the most beautiful thing she had ever seen on earth but she knew they were from the heavens. That these colors were like the songs of the ancients' spirits. I remembered all this while I was standing out there in the cold, but I had forgotten the cold, and as I looked at these waves of blue and gold and even purple, I felt the touch of Mama someplace deep in my spirit. I could even hear her voice clearly, as if it spilled from those curtains of color right down to me. This is the first time I have thought of my mother without sadness, without sharp pain. I am glad that I was born to her, that I was on earth for twelve years with her.

Captain Lewis explained to me that the stars do not move separately but together, and he explained how the earth turns around the sun so it is as if the earth is another star in the sliding land above we call the heavens. I look up at this sky beating with strange light that wraps me up in its cloth of colors and I think we are all parts of this single piece—white men, half-breeds, Arikara, Mandan, Teton Sioux, mud trout, barking squirrel, Charley Floyd, Silverwing Woman. We are all part of this slow starry dance. Oh, Silverwing Woman, you are here!

November 7, 1804

That Charbonneau is a real noisome, loud man. But I figured out why the Captains want him: He's got two

Indian wives. The one called Sacajawea is Shoshoni. She was captured by the Hidatsa, a nearby tribe. Then Charbonneau bought her from them as a wife. So she knows French as well as Shoshoni. She is the wife who will be traveling with us. We shall be heading into Shoshoni country in the spring. And after the trouble with the Teton Sioux, the Captains want a good translator. I think she's just a year older than me. I saw her yesterday for the first time. She's got a baby coming on. So I guess this means we'll be traveling next spring with a papoose!

November 9, 1804

Ice in the river today.

November 10, 1804

There are a lot of French traders from Canada around here. Charbonneau is not the only Frenchman. There are trappers and traders, some with Indian wives also, like Jessaume. There is another named Larocque. So I hear a lot of French. They don't speak the fine kind like Father Dumaine. It sounds rough and as if it's coming out their nose rather than their mouth, but I can understand it.

November 12, 1805

Woke up this morning and the whole world was frosted. Every pine needle bristled in its little icy jacket, and then fog swirled through the camp. The squaw of one of the chiefs, Big White, from the lower Mandan village came up the path. Thought it was a frosted boulder on legs until I realized that she was bent over with a pack. I ran up and helped take it off her back. It was close to a hundred pounds of meat sent by the chief. When this old squaw looked up at me, she had picks of ice hanging from her hair and her eyebrows were stiff with frost. I noticed that she had some red paint in her ears. Lots of the women have it when they come into the fort. I think this red paint is a kind of special decoration they sometimes put on. Maybe they just wear it when they come to see us, because when we saw the families in the bull boats, none of the women had red paint in their ears.

Later: Well, we thought the red paint in the squaws' ears was strange. However, when the one-eyed Hidatsa chief came, he thought York had done painted himself. He licked his fingers and tried to wipe York's color off. He was really surprised when York stayed black.

November 13, 1804

I spent the whole day moving provisions from the storage cabin of the keelboat into the storehouse. About midday Charbonneau's wives came along. I was mistaken. He's got three. One is called Otter Woman, the other Corn Woman, and then there is Sacajawea, which means Bird Woman. She's the one who's going to be having a baby. You can tell. They all had their ears painted red on the inside and a stripe of red where they parted their hair. They stood around and watched and giggled and explained their names to us through French and sign language. Sacajawea didn't giggle much. She just watched. Then Charbonneau came up and started yelling at them in a mixture of French and Hidatsa. Corn Woman and Otter Woman looked scared, but not Sacajawea. For the first time I even saw a trace of a smile from her. She kind of ambled along real slow behind them. Charbonneau turned around and yelled, "*Dépêche-toi, dépêche-toi, tu idiote.*" I understood what he said. "Hurry up, idiot." But she didn't hurry at all. She was too busy looking at how we were refitting a joist beam on the floor of one of the huts.

Later: Shannon came and got me to come to the meeting with the Captains and Charbonneau and his wives. Pierre and Francis are out hunting and they want someone who understands French. Here's how it works: the Captains speak to Charbonneau in English and he talks to his wife in Hidatsa, but they are worried that Charbonneau might not understand the English, so I am supposed to be there, handy with the French. When I get there Otter Woman and Corn Woman are looking at their faces in a mirror the Captains gave them, laughing and pointing, but Sacajawea, she's not looking at the mirror. Her eyes are roving around and I can tell she is really studying the Captains. Captain Clark said, "Have your wife tell us of her people." Then Charbonneau translates and Sacajawea says something and Charbonneau explodes at her in a mixture of French and Hidatsa. I can understand the French. "Not the Minnetaree, *idiote femme*, the people you were born to, the Shoshoni," he yells at her. Then she looks at him and begins to speak. She slips in a few French words so I understood, too. She is talking about a land of shining mountains and where the people go in the summer and then in the winter. The most important word she says is *chevaux*. Horses. They have horses. Many horses.

November 18, 1804

Captain Lewis's thermometer says it is 12 degrees below zero, but it is not too cold for him to get out his sextant and quadrant and the rest of his observing gear. It is so cold we had to oil the sextant to get the arms to slide. In any case we worked a good hour or two, including the mathematics calculations, and we figure that the latitude of our fort is 44.08 degrees north and the longitude is

99.39 degrees west. So we have traveled sixteen hundred miles from the mouth of the Missouri.

November 21, 1804

The Captains are worried that all these plans for peace 'mongst the Indian tribes might not work out like President Jefferson hopes. Seems the Indians don't care about some Great White Father back in a place called Washington. Warriors from Black Cat's village, the second Mandan village farther up the river, came today to say that the Sioux had practically killed two Arikara who had come to talk peace. Then there was a rumor that we, the Corps, had joined in with the Sioux. Captain Clark thinks that one was started by the Mandans themselves to keep the Hidatsa away. They got worried when they saw Charbonneau and his wives up here. You see, the Captains have been telling all these Indians that they're going to set up a big trading post here, maybe as soon as next year, at the fort. The Mandans want to take the hog's share of any trading that might go on. That's why they want to spook the Hidatsa away. It's not good. They'll end up stirring up trouble between everyone.

Started snowing heavily tonight.

November 27, 1804

Still snowing. River running with ice.

I talked with Sacajawea this morning. She understands a fair amount of French. Between French and sign language we did pretty well. She had heard about Antoine, and she asked me if she could bring Otter Woman's little boy Tess over to see him. I said sure.

Later: Sacajawea and little Tess, he's about three, came by. They were much impressed with Antoine. I let Tess feed him some grain pellets. That gal Sacajawea, her eyes never rest. She took in everything about that little critter. Then she started looking around the hut where we have all the specimens and the scientific equipment. Pretty soon she wanted to know about everything. It's not easy explaining these things in English or French, let alone sign language and the couple of words I know of Hidatsa. I try the best I can.

November 30, 1804

We are on full alert at the fort. News came last evening of a Sioux and Arikara raid on five Mandan hunters. The Captains are in an upset. Here they are selling themselves as peacemakers and I guess no one is listening. Captain Lewis organizes our guards here at the fort. Captain Clark set out to help the Mandans. But the snow is deep.

December 7, 1804

A Mandan chief showed up today to report large numbers of buffalo about two miles away. We were invited to go on a chase. Lewis chose fifteen men, including, of course, his best shots. The chief offered up horses. I wasn't chosen. Just as they were about to leave I ran up to Captain Lewis and just plain asked. He turned around and raised his eyebrows as if in surprise. I wasn't sure whether it was surprise because I had dared to ask or what. He said, "Why, sure, Gus." It was more like he was surprised he hadn't thought to ask me. So sometimes it pays to just plain ask. Then he told me to run back and get his sextant and the cro-no-meter and a few other instruments. I had never seen the likes of this in my life. I couldn't believe how those Mandans can ride—and through five feet of snow. They ride bareback and guide the horses simply by shifting their weight and pressing with their knees. Their hands are free for shooting arrows. And can they shoot! Eleven buffalo were brought down, eight by the Mandan hunters. They got such a whack out of those bows that the arrows often went straight through the buffalo.

My hands are so cold I can hardly write. But Captain Lewis is fiddling with the dang quadrant. It done froze up. So I'm waiting for him. In the meantime the snow has turned red with the blood of the buffalo. The squaws who followed us on foot have set about butchering. I want to tell you that there are no tougher labors than those of a Mandan squaw. The little old one who came with the hundred pounds of meat the other day, by gum, she's out there hopping over these huge humps of buffalo like a grasshopper. Cold doesn't seem to bother them that much. When one of them noticed I was shivering, she took me over to the buffalo she was butchering and told me to stick my hands into the steaming guts. When I backed off, the other squaws giggled, shoved me forward, and yanked on my arms until I was buried up to my elbows in guts. I wiped them off so I wouldn't get my writing messed up, but now they're cold again!

December 9, 1804

Captain Lewis loved the buffalo hunt so much we stayed out all night. I thought I'd die when I heard he wanted to stay out but I couldn't complain, as I had asked to come. We slept wrapped up in buffalo robes. We survived, that's all I can say. Captain Lewis took the temperature at daybreak. Forty-five degrees below zero. When he said that my eyeballs froze on the spot.

December 10, 1804

Warming up. Forty-three below zero! York says spring is just around the corner. Then he laughs. York looks right peculiar in all this snow, him being so big and black. He doesn't like to wear a hat. So sometimes if the snow flurries are coming down gentle, they sort of frost his short, kinky hair along with his eyebrows and his eyelashes and he looks fantastic. The Indian children love him. And the squaws, too. They think he's magic. I think he's magic, too, when he comes so black, into the tent all sprinkled with snow.

December 15, 1804

Feeling poorly this evening. I don't want to tell Captain Lewis. I see his store of medical supplies and it sets fear on me. Lancets for bleeding. Dr. Rush's Thunderclappers that blast everything but your soul out of your body. The last thing I want to do is get treated by Captain Lewis. Not that he's a bad doctor, but the remedies scare the daylights out of me.

December 30, 1804

I been sick as a dog. So sick I didn't even mind when Captain Lewis started his doctoring. I was half out of my head. They gave me seventeen drops of laudanum, then a dose of saltpeter, then pumped me full of sage tea. Finally they done made a poultice out of that bark they used for snakebite and mixed it up with something that smelled peppery hot. When they laid that on my chest it felt like my lungs were going to jump right out.

December 31, 1804

Sacajawea came to visit me today. I could hardly believe it. She has learned a few English words. She said, "River Eye Boy?" Then she sort of smiled shy and covered her mouth. I say "Who you talking to?" Then she points. And I say "Me?" And she nods. "Why River Eye Boy?" She tries to explain, mostly in sign language. She makes the sign for river, which is the sign for water. She put her right hand over her face and points her first finger straight. Next she makes the sign for small. So I know it wasn't the Missouri. It takes about five minutes, but I finally get it. There's a smaller river up a piece where the water runs a blue-green color. That is the color of my eyes. So I guess that's why she calls me River Eye Boy. She tells me that the fishing is good in that river and when the ice melts she'll take me there when she goes to catch fish. Then she gets up to leave and she draws out a real smooth stone from under her blanket. And says, "River stone for River Eyes." I guess it's a stone from the river. It's black with swirls of white. It kind of looks like a starry night. Imagine that. A rock that reminds you of the sky. I think this is the first present anyone has ever given me aside from my mama.

When Sacajawea got up I could see that the baby is growing really big. She had trouble hoisting herself up.

January 1, 1805

First day of the new year. Most of the company went over to the lower Mandan village. The Captains had told them it was a holiday for white men, so they were invited to sing and dance. Captain Lewis wouldn't let me go. Said I was too weak.

January 5, 1805

I am well enough to go to the Buffalo Dance in the Mandan village that the Indians invited us to. There is music and dancing, and all the Indian men are all dressed up in their best feathers and paint. The hunters make a circle and their women are behind them. In the Buffalo Dance the wives of hunters go up practically stark naked and kiss and hug the old men. The Mandans believe that in some way the old men have a special power and they pass it to the women and this makes the buffalo come near.

January 10, 1804

Seems like every day some Mandan shows up to be doc-
tored by Captain Lewis. A few days ago a woman brought
in her young girl with a big boil on her back. She swapped
him corn for the doctoring. He lanced the boil and put
a poultice on it. That bark again. Today a Mandan boy
showed with his feet froze. The Captain soaked the boy's
feet in cold water first. It usually works but I'm not sure
if it's going to work this time. That boy's toes looked kind
of gray when they come out of the water.

January 16, 1805

We keep hearing more and more about how the Shoshoni,
or the Snake Indians—Sacajawea's people—have big
herds of horses. A chief of the people the French call Big
Bellies, or *Gros Ventres*, came today full of talk about how
he and his nation were going to make war on the Shoshoni
because of all the horses. Somehow the Captains discour-
aged him. They gave the Big Speech again and promised
that the Great White Father in Washington would pro-
tect them and that more was to be gained by chasing after
peace than war.

January 20, 1805

Sacajawea came to camp today with that husband of hers. I don't know how she stands him. Somehow she docs. When he yells at her, her eyes just grow far away. But Captain Clark really blew up at Charbonneau when he yelled at her today. He told him to watch his mouth and that he'd just as soon take Sacajawea without him than with him when we leave in the spring and head for the sea. I saw Charbonneau grow pale under his whiskers. The Captains have given Charbonneau and his wives a hut in the fort where they can stay whenever they want. This is especially good, as Captain Lewis wants Sacajawea nearby as her time for birthing draws close.

January 21, 1805

Sacajawea and Charbonneau spent the night in camp in their hut. This morning Charbonneau went off with the Captains to check on the big keelboat that is pretty much frozen in the ice. They're trying to figure out how to free it up. I was in the storeroom going over our specimens when Sacajawea came in. She is very interested in all the scientific equipment. We can talk pretty good between our French and the sign language, and now I have learned some more Hidatsa words. Suddenly she got this faraway, sad look in her eye when she was looking at the stuffed badger we're sending back to President Jefferson. I thought it couldn't be a dead badger making her look this sad, even though we'd done a pretty good job of making this fellow look awfully like life itself. I didn't know what to say. So finally I blurted out in French and sign language, "You sad about that badger?" and she said, *"Pas exactement,"* which means "not exactly." Then she said, and I'll do the best to explain it, that this badger seemed to her not quite dead and not quite alive but caught between what she calls the living world, this earth, and the Camps of the Dead, meaning heaven. Then she said very quietly, *"Comme moi, exactement!"* — "Like me, exactly." And I knew in that instant what she meant. You see, Sacajawea was kidnapped by the Minnetaree from her people, the Shoshoni, when she was about eight years old. Then she was sold to the Hidatsas in this region. Then she was bought by Charbonneau. She has lived in so many worlds that there is not one that feels like home. She is caught somewhere between nations and camps. She is like the badger, forever stuck between worlds, and like the badger she feels she is not quite alive and not quite dead. But then she patted her huge belly and said, "This is my life." I felt so sad that night for Sacajawea. I prayed to God that she find her home. Then I prayed something really bad that if I were back in St. Charles I would have to go to confession for, but there ain't no confessional out here in Mandan country by this frozen river. I prayed that Charbonneau would die.

January 26, 1805

Lots of doctoring going on today. The boy with the frozen toes came back. They had turned black, so Captain Lewis sawed them off. The boy didn't hardly whimper. Another man came in with pleurisy real bad. The Captain bled him and greased his chest and slapped a bark poultice on it.

February 4, 1805

We've just about run out of meat. I keep looking for that bent little old squaw to come up the path with the hundred pounds of meat she brought before but she ain't coming. Captain Clark set out with a hunting party today and Captain Lewis had a real good idea. He's putting John Shields to work with the bellows and a forge. Private Shields was a blacksmith back where he came from. He's going to start making axes, battle-axes, the kind the Indians like for war. And he's mending stuff for them too, in trade for meat. I think it's kind of funny that here the Captains are always giving the Big Speech about how the Great White Father wants peace, but when we want meat we make battle-axes for these folks. I said something to York about this and he just shook his head and laughed, saying, "Why you surprised, boy? Half the time white folks don't make no sense at all."

February 6, 1805

We didn't get meat for the battle-axes. We got corn. Guess it will have to do.

February 11, 1805

Sacajawea went into labor last night, but Captain Lewis says the baby is moving slow and painful. She is having a really tough time, I guess. She is down there at Charbonneau's hut. I wandered down there around mid-day, and I didn't hear her screaming then, just groaning and panting. Later Jessaume came to Captain Lewis and said we got to get some rattles from some rattlesnakes. Captain Lewis said I could take the rattles off a specimen we had killed. So Jessaume and I went back to where we kept the specimens, and I chopped off rattles from this big old rattler we killed last fall. He ground them up into a near powder and took the powder back to the hut. He put it in some water or tea or something. Well, it wasn't more than ten minutes before I heard a baby's cry, and it weren't no whimper. It was a loud holler. You would have thought that baby had been bitten by the rattler. Anyhow Sacajawea has got herself a fine fat little baby boy. They named him Jean Baptiste Charbonneau and that old reprobate Charbonneau went all over the fort crowing like he'd given birth himself. It's funny. When that little baby yowled, I noticed that every man around the fort got a soft look in his eye as if each one was remembering some little kid brother or sister they had left behind. We've seen a lot of babies along this endless river and heard a lot, too, but a baby's cry right in our own camp, well, that is something special.

February 12, 1805

Last night the mercury dropped to nearly fifty below. Seaman has taken to crawling in the sack with me on cold nights. Can't say I mind. I hope little Jean Baptiste don't feel the cold. He is a cute little fellow. I went and visited him today. He's a real coppery red color and got a lick of black hair that won't lie flat, right on top of his head. I think he's going to be just like his mother. He watches every thing the same way she does with his dark eyes. He almost seems like he is all eyes to me.

February 17, 1805

Captain Lewis can be so dang stubborn. Sometimes I just hate it when he gets an idea fixed in his head, but that's exactly what he's done. He decided that those Sioux and Arikara who attacked the Mandans a few weeks before had to be taught a lesson. So he set out with twenty-four of us. The weather was awful—deep snow, ice, howling winds. By the end of the first day we all had torn-up, bleeding feet. The trail of those Sioux and the Arikara went dead cold, but would Lewis stop? No, sir. He pushed on. We covered thirty miles, only to find a few old abandoned Sioux tipis. Finally he gave up today and we went hunting. We're having good luck so far. Three elk and a deer.

February 18, 1805

Take it back what I said about Captain Lewis. Because he pushed on we've done got ourselves almost a ton of meat. This is real good because we are all sick to death of corn.

February 25, 1805

I go every chance I get to play with little Jean Baptiste. Captain Clark loves him, too. Sacajawea nicknamed him Pomp. Pomp means "leader of men" in Shoshoni. He's a smart little feller. You can just tell. I made up a rattle stick for him with colorful beads. If I swing it slowly over his face from one side to another, he can follow it ever so well with his eyes. Sacajawea and I think up a lot of little games to play with him. Charbonneau hardly pays any attention to the baby now that it's here. That's fine by my sights. This baby ain't going to learn nothing but bragging from that fool father of his.

March 3, 1805

Even though it is only the third day of the new month something is stirring in the air. There's a different slant to the sun and new warmth in its light. I feel it. Sacajawea says she's going to make me a new pair of moccasins. Mine are just about worn out.

March 4, 1805

I am busy every day packing things to send when the keelboat heads back down the river to St. Louis. We shall send back at least a hundred or more different specimens—animals, soil, rocks. I spent all afternoon labeling Captain Lewis's mineral samples— everything from pebbles common to the Missouri to pumice stone, lava chips, quartz, Glauber's salts, and alum. Never knew what any of these were until he started me looking for them. Then there's skins of mice, all sorts of birds, and skeletons of pronghorn goats. I don't know where they're going to put all this stuff back in Washington. It'll probably bring in a whole swarm of fleas to the White House. I can just see the next big fancy dinner and everyone itching and scratching themselves to death.

I still don't know whether I am part of the permanent party or not. I was able to forget about it through most of the winter, but now as I pack these things, I think about it all the time. I look at Antoine and I think, "Are you and I going to be river brothers or not? I sure hope not." You'd think I'd get up my nerve to ask. But I just don't know how.

March 6, 1805

Sacajawea was talking about how happy she is about heading off in a few weeks toward the land of her people. Well, I just came straight out and told her what's on my mind and how I don't know whether or not I'll be going and how much I want to see the ocean. Talking isn't hard at all for us anymore. She looked kind of surprised when I told her all this. She said, "River Eyes, I am sure you will be going. Who will help the Captain with his marks on paper?" That's what she calls writing, marks on paper. "And who will help him with his star-making pictures?" That's what she calls taking sights for longitude and latitude. I just shrugged. She asked why I don't ask. And I shrugged again and said I didn't know how to ask. Then her eyes grew fierce. "River Eyes, you're being a foolish one. You have words in your tongue and on your fingers. You can speak and you can make signs in air and word marks on paper. You are like a fat man eating buffalo hump while complaining about being hungry and skinny. You go ask, silly boy." I told her I would think on it. She said, "Don't think on it. Go ask."

March 7, 1805

Haven't got my nerve up to ask yet, and now I can't go see Sacajawea because she'll ask if I asked.

March 8, 1805

Met Sacajawea coming up the trail to the fort. She glared at me, then shook her head because she knew I hadn't asked yet.

March 9, 1805

Truly, that Sacajawea can glare. I think she's teaching little Pomp to glare, too, because he gave me a right mean dirty look for a baby.

March 10, 1805

I asked—I'm going!!! I am part of the permanent party of the Corps of Discovery. I can't believe I thought it would be so hard. And the funny part is that Captain Lewis looked so surprised when I asked. He said, "You actually thought you wouldn't be going the whole way? You're the only person who writes a decent hand in the entire outfit. It's probably one of the best and most practical things those fool Jesuits ever did—teach you to read and write."

I am glad Father Dumaine didn't hear him. Captain Lewis don't set much store by religion, particularly the Catholic Church. Just like him to think that the whole reason for a religion is to teach this half-breed to write so he could help Captain Meriwether Lewis discover a continent. Nothing about God or Jesus suffering on the cross or serving Jesus—just about serving Captain Lewis. But the Captain is a good man no matter what he thinks about religion. It's really how he acts that counts. And he acts like a good, decent man.

March 11, 1805

Just when I think everything is going to be perfect that dang Charbonneau messes everything up. The Captain done kicked him and Sacajawea out of the fort because

Charbonneau tried to be so high and mighty with the Captain when they sat down to work out the contract for him and Sacajawea. Charbonneau wanted so much money. Then he said he wouldn't stand guard. He wouldn't cook. He wouldn't hunt. The Captain told him to take his wives and kids back to their dang hut down the river.

March 15, 1805

Message from Charbonneau today in which he asked the Captains to "excuse his simplicity and to take him into service." I see Sacajawea behind this. There was no way she was going to miss seeing her people.

March 17, 1805

Charbonneau showed up today with just Sacajawea. He was as tame as a pussycat, and if I thought Sacajawea glared at me, you should have seen her eyes on Charbonneau. They bore through him like lead slugs from a Kentucky rifle.

March 25, 1805

Ice in the river has been breaking up for the past two days. Every day great hunks of it come floating down along with uprooted trees and today a buffalo carcass. The Indians jump from one cake to another. It looks like a dance to see them hopping up, down, and across the river on these chunks of ice.

March 27, 1805

We're all working hard repairing the keelboat and building new canoes. The keelboat and the two old canoes will head downriver again in about a week. Then we'll start off into territory where they say no white men have gone, not even the French traders. After a piece we'll come to the headwaters of the Missouri and then finally to the western ocean, the Shining Sea.

Captain Lewis talked to me today about starting a dictionary of all the Indian words. This will become really important, he says, when we get into Shoshoni country. He wants the Hidatsa words written down and then the Shoshoni words for those same Hidatsa words and then the English. He says President Jefferson has this idea about Indian languages and being able to trace the origins of their nations and tribes through their language. Captain Lewis knows that Sacajawea and I get on well and that I have learned a lot of Hidatsa this winter. He is hoping that she will explain the Shoshoni words to me. He flat out said that he would like to keep Charbonneau out of it as much as possible because he doesn't trust him, even though the man does speak fair Hidatsa.

April 5, 1805

Put the keelboat back in the water today for the first time. We freed her up from the ice, along with the six new canoes. York and I paddled one of the new canoes out into the stream. She was lively as a fish out there in the current. Of course, she'll hunker down and be steadier when we load her up, but she's tight and with her comely lines will slice right through the cold water.

April 6, 1805

Can't sleep tonight. Tomorrow we leave and I am so excited. I try to imagine the end of this river. I try to imagine the western ocean and I can't. The Captains have been busy all day writing letters home that shall be carried down the river all the way to St. Louis. Captain Lewis has a mother and several brothers and sisters. Some of them are half brothers. Captain Clark has a large family, too. All the men are writing to their families, except York and me. I don't know who I would write. Oh, Lordy! Just thought of it. Father Dumaine! I guess he'll finally get the idea that I am not cut out to be a priest.

April 8, 1805

We set off yesterday about four o'clock in the afternoon with our eight vessels—two old pirogues and six new canoes. I have never seen Captain Lewis happier. And last night as I transcribed his journals I began to understand more completely the grandness of this venture. I copy now here some of what I copied into his journal.

"This little fleet altho not quite so respectable as those of Columbus or Captain Cook, were still viewed by us with as much pleasure as those deservedly famous adventurers ever beheld theirs . . . we were now about to penetrate a country at least two thousand miles in width, on which the foot of civilized man had never trodden."

I had heard of Columbus, but I ain't never heard of this Captain Cook. So I asked and Captain Lewis told me that he was a great English sea captain who had, in Lewis's own words, "explored more of the earth's surface than any other man." He sailed the Pacific and as far north toward the pole as the ice would permit him and as far south so as to round the Cape of the Horn of the great southern continent of America and he discovered islands and new oceans. But the tips of those continents, those faraway islands, are to me no more imaginable than the end of this river.

April 9, 1805

Except for the Captains, Sacajawea, the baby Pomp, Charbonneau, and Drouillard, we all sleep in the open. They share a skin tent in the style of the Indians, a buffalo hide stretched over a frame of alder and soft pine limbs. They also ride together in the white pirogue, along with Cruzatte, except the Captains often walk along the shore or Drouillard goes off hunting. Sacajawea has already made herself very useful. She has taught us about a new food—artichoke buds. The mice hoard them and she took a stick and dug them up. She seems to know just where to dig. When boiled they make a tender, tasty dish. Charbonneau does nothing.

April 11, 1805

We have covered nearly ninety miles in these past four days, and today, for the first time since the curve at the Great Bend of the river near the mouth of the Kansas, this long river turns directly west once again. The country on both sides of the river sweeps on immense plains as far as the eye can see. There is not a single tree in sight, but herds of elk and buffalo and antelope graze on the sea of grass.

April 13, 1805

Captain Lewis shot a huge goose today. It has a white belly but its wings are a pretty patchwork of brown and black feathers. He climbed a tree to examine its nest and brought back an egg. He calls it a Canada goose. I have been measuring and weighing it and the egg. I think he just plans to skin this goose and not stuff it. Also today we saw our first signs of the great grizzly bears we have been told so much about. The Indians say these bears stand more than ten feet tall and weigh as much as our keelboat when loaded. They are savage and have great fanged teeth.

April 17, 1805

I think I have suddenly grown. My trousers hit me well above the anklebone. This morning my shirt split open on my back and even the sleeves feel tight. Sacajawea says she will make me a new one. She has a supply of hide. The moccasins she made me are the best I have ever worn. They are very soft but tough. She says that is because she chews the skins so well before she sews them. I am not only bigger but much stronger. I can tell from paddling. There are six blades or paddles to a canoe. I know that my pull is equal to that of any man I paddle with. We met with a strong but confusing eddy yesterday that threatened to sweep us into a pile of brush floating downriver. I pulled with all my might. I could feel the strength of my paddle against the current.

At night we are all hugely hungry and eat our fill of meat, as it is so abundant. Captain Lewis estimates that each man eats as much as eight or nine pounds of meat a day. The beaver tail and its liver are everyone's favorite and this is beaver-rich country. Some of the men begin to trap on their own when they get a chance, for the pelts pull a pretty price back in St. Louis.

April 18, 1805

I think the Captains are going to stop the private beaver trapping. A big fight broke out between two men over a trapped beaver. Each thought it was his trap that caught the beaver.

April 19, 1805

We lay by today, because the wind is so strong out of the northwest that we could never paddle against it. I played with Pomp. Pomp holds things now if you put them in his hand, and he is starting to reach out for stuff a little bit. So I made some more rattles for him. I told Sacajawea that we could weigh Pomp on one of the scales that Captain Lewis uses for weighing his specimens. She got very excited about this. So we took Pomp over and I set up the scales. Pomp weighs a whopping twelve pounds. Sacajawea was so pleased. I showed her how to write the number twelve and then I said it to her in English and French. Then she told me the word in Hidatsa and Shoshoni.

April 20, 1805

I went walking out into the countryside with Captain Clark today. He invited me. It was a good day not to be on the river, as a bank caved in and nearly swamped one of the canoes. However, Captain Clark and I made an interesting discovery. As we were walking along we saw what looked like a long bundle on the ground. When we approached we realized it was a dead Indian woman wrapped up in hides that had been laced tightly and placed in a sled. Alongside the sled was her dead dog. I had been told that the Indians in this country scaffold their dead. They put them on high platforms, which they carry up into trees or on stilts if there are no trees. Captain Clark and I examined the arrangement carefully. Numerous trinkets were wrapped into the lacings, along with a leather pouch of different colored earth paints. The bones of small animals were also tucked in, including the still-feathered body of a blue jay. It was clear that the scaffolding had collapsed.

April 25, 1805

Captain Lewis is most upset. Seaman has disappeared. The Captain was low enough before this happened. Now he is truly in despair.

Later: Seaman walked into camp at eight o'clock this morning. The Captain ran to the dog and embraced him. We get under way. It is a bitter cold morning for this late in April and the water freezes to our oars, but by this evening we have almost reached the river that the Indians call the Yellowstone.

April 26, 1805

Captain Lewis sent Joe Field to explore a few miles up the Yellowstone. I was to accompany the Captain, as he had many astronomical sights he wanted to make. We measured the altitude of the sun all day long until the clouds rolled in. All this is important to the Captain because he wants to precisely mark the longitude of the Missouri River and where it joins the Yellowstone. Joe Field came back and said that the Yellowstone is a wandering sort of river with many twists and turns and sandbars.

May 8, 1805

Every day we've been naming things—new rivers, creeks, streams, bluffs. Two days ago we came upon a small river feeding into the Missouri on the north bank. There were so many porcupines that Captain Lewis has named it the Porcupine River. Then there is another river that the Minnetaree Indians call the River-that-Scolds-All-the-Others, but Captain Lewis changed its name to the Milk River because of the light color of its water.

I went walking with Sacajawea and Charbonneau and Drouillard today. Sacajawea found wild licorice and a mess of other roots called white apples.

May 9, 1805

Charbonneau finally earned his keep today. He made a kind of sausage called *boudin blanc*. Captain Lewis wrote out the whole recipe for it.

May 11, 1805

Private Bratton, whom I never took as a flighty fellow, came running down the bank late this afternoon, flailing his arms and screaming his head off. I thought he'd been attacked by a nest of hornets. But it wasn't hornets. It was a grizzly. He'd shot and wounded one. Thought he got him right in the chest but dang if that bear didn't turn and give him chase. Captain Lewis doesn't cotton to the idea of a member of the Corps being shown up by a bear, even a grizzly. So he ordered a canoe put in and for the men "to give pursuit in quest of the monster," which is just a fancy way of saying, "We're going on a bear hunt." I was not asked to join. They did, however, find this bear. Bratton's bullets had gone through its lungs, but the bear was still running. They finally cornered him and shot the monster through the head twice.

May 13, 1805

I keep patting myself today. I can't quite believe I am all here because it's just short of a miracle that parts of me aren't floating around in the gut of a grizzly bear. Here is what happened. I was in a canoe with Labiche and Reuben and Joseph Field, and we had just landed on a small beach because Reuben thought that he saw some movement in the brush and that it was deer. Well, he thought wrong. It wasn't deer. It was the biggest grizzly ever! Least, biggest I'd seen. It rose out of the brush and looked not ten feet tall but twenty. It was a monster! It opened its jaws and roared and the sun blazed off the biggest, sharpest teeth this side of hell. Reuben fired and I saw something spit off the bear's shoulder. But that didn't slow the bear, who began to charge. Reuben was off to one side and hied himself into the brush. Joseph and Labiche still each had a foot in the canoe. But it was me who was right in that bear's sights, directly between him and the water. Joseph and Labiche pushed off from shore and I almost made it into the canoe but fell into the water. Labiche reached for me but couldn't grab me, and before you know it the canoe had swirled away into the current and I felt this warm rush of air on the back of my head and it was the breath of that bear not five feet from me, those teeth just glinting and its eyes rolled back in its head. All I could think was, Duck! Duck under the water! So I took a huge gulp of air and dove. It wasn't that deep and I swear I felt that bear's claw on my moccasin. I scraped my chin on the rocky bottom but I just kept swimming. Go deep! Go deep! The words pounded in my head. Maybe that bear won't smell me if I'm deep. Maybe he can't see. Maybe he'll think I have just plain up and disappeared.

Now my lungs felt that they're about to burst. But I just got to keep swimming underwater until I get to the deep part and the current. Finally I can't stand it another second. I think to myself, Now what's worse, burst lungs or being chomped by a bear? Then my head bumps something. Not real hard but I see a shadow that looks like wings and a long upcurved crest just like a silverwing swift. And I think of my mother, Silverwing Woman.

That's my last thought. I can almost see her face floating down through the shots of sunlight in the water. I reach up and my hand feels a big snag of branches. I break through the surface and my face is whipped by limbs. It's a whole tree pulled roots and all from a river bank cave-in. I couldn't have done better if I had climbed a tree. It's the perfect hideaway. I look back and I see the bear swimming, turning his head this way and that like he's looking for me. Then I heard another shot. The air splatters with blood. And the bear sinks. It was Joseph Field from the canoe. I wave to them from my floating tree and they circled back pick me up.

So here I sit, drying off in the sun and patting myself. It's a marvel, every square inch of flesh that's right here on my bones and not in that bear's gut, I think. And I keep thinking the ways of the Lord are indeed mysterious, and even more mysterious is that shadow of the silverwing swift and the face of my mother in the sunlit water.

May 14, 1805

As if the bear didn't give enough excitement yesterday this morning a squall hit. The white pirogue was under sail and Charbonneau was at the helm. He should have turned her before the wind but the fool headed her into it. I was on the banks and watched as the canoe was laid over flat on her side by the wind slamming down the river. She righted but was filled with water, and Charbonneau, who can't swim, was crying and praying to whatever god he prays to. He never once looked to Sacajawea or little Pomp. All I could think was that they would drown. I started tearing down the bank toward the swamped canoe. I saw Cruzatte in the bow level a rifle at Charbonneau in the stern and heard him bark, "Grab hold that rudder or I'll shoot your cursed head off." This brought Charbonneau to his senses. Meanwhile I heard Captain Lewis come up behind me and heard this terrible gasp for what he saw was all manner of equipment and articles, including valuable instruments, and even some of the journals floating about in the swirling water. But then I saw that while others in the canoe were bailing out the water, Sacajawea was leaning far out and grabbing whatever she could of these articles. She was as calm as if she were bathing her baby, who was still strapped to her back. I think if Captain Lewis had not spied her doing this he would have plunged directly into the river to save the articles, for he had already begun to unbutton his coat.

May 15, 1805

Here is what Captain Lewis wrote about Sacajawea last evening in his journal, concerning the disaster on the river yesterday. "The Indian woman to whom I ascribe equal fortitude and resolution with any person on board at the time of the accident, caught and preserved most of the light articles which were washed overboard." He wrote nothing about Charbonneau, but he called him into his tent last night and in a voice as icy as the river told the man that he was a fool and a coward and not deserving of the wife he had. I don't believe I have ever in my life heard anything as ice cold as that low, steady voice of Captain Lewis. I think I would endure five hundred lashes of the whip on my bare back before I would ever want that voice directed toward me.

May 16, 1805

Today is a special day. Captain Clark let me name a falls. We had come upon a little falls on the north bank of the river. It spilled down in a silver cord from some high black rocks that were sprigged with the creeping juniper that we have taken a cutting of to send home. These were the prettiest little falls I have ever seen. And I have named them Silverwing Falls for my mother. Captain Clark let me mark the spot on the map and write in the letters myself. For me there was something almost holy about this marking down. Then the Captain shook my hand. I felt that this was as sacred as when Father

Dumaine lays the wafer on my tongue during communion. I went back out to the falls this evening at twilight and took a long drink of their clear water. I looked up at the soaring timbers on either side that framed a piece of the sky. The sky was exactly the color of a peach. I have seen only one peach in my life, but this sky was pink and golden and then this silver cord of water fell from the dark rock. I thought, This is church enough for me. I felt that God being stand-up, like I know Him to be, understood and thought it fine. You don't have to be between four walls to pray.

May 19, 1805

Reuben Field shot a beaver today and Seaman jumped in the water to retrieve it. Bad luck! The beaver wasn't dead. Still had plenty of fight in him and sank his teeth into Seaman's hind leg, cutting an artery. Captain Lewis has had a fearsome time trying to stop the bleeding. I hope the old dog makes it.

May 20, 1805

We have entered a most desertlike region of the country. The river begins to turn south on its course. We passed a creek swarming with bugs. We named it Blowing Fly Creek.

Seaman still very weak.

There is another stream. Its waters run clear and lively, and I am most happy to write that the Captains have decided to call it Bird Woman's River after Sacajawea.

May 23, 1805

Every day we see and name new things. There is now a Shields' River and a York's Dry Fork. And yes, there is a Gus's Divide where the river splits for a mile before the two strands rejoin.

Seaman is much improved today. He was even able to limp about a bit.

May 24, 1805

We think we might see some mountains far in the distance, like pale white ghosts against the sky.

May 25, 1805

We do most definitely see the mountains. Can the river's end be far?

May 29, 1805

Well, Seaman is completely recovered. He proved himself this morning. We heard a bellow just at daybreak that
shook the entire camp. Before I know it I see this hurl
ing dark mass. It was a buffalo bull come charging right
through camp. He just about trampled the Field brothers. Seaman bolted out of the Captain's tent and dang if
he didn't charge that buffalo and chase him right out of
camp. We named the nearby stream Bull Creek. I think
we should have named it Seaman's Creek myself.

It's been four days since we saw those mountains, and
they don't seem to be getting any closer. The water of the
river is getting shallower, and often we must get out and
pull the canoes. The water is icy cold but the sun on our
backs hot. So you freeze one end and fry the other.

May 30, 1805

We started to smell something fierce and awful today.
Then when we rounded the bend we saw a mountain of
buffalo piled up in the river. Captain Lewis thinks it's
what he calls a "pishkin" or buffalo jump. Captain Lewis
and I both heard from some Hidatsa how young Indian
boys dressed in buffalo robes would lure buffalos to their
death at the edge of a cliff while other Indians chased
them from the rear. The only problem, as I pointed out

to Captain Lewis, is that there is no cliff here. So now we think that maybe they tried to cross the river in the winter and broke through the ice and drowned. Whatever it was it sure does stink now. Captain Lewis named the creek flowing in here Slaughter Creek.

May 31, 1805

Captain Clark came upon a stream this day and named it the Judith River. I guess he has a sweetheart back home by the name of Judith. It's awful close to Slaughter Creek. I think if I were naming a river for a sweetheart, I would have put a little more distance between it and those stinking buffalo.

June 1, 1805

We have entered a most fantastical part of the country. White cliffs soar up around us, twisting into all sorts of shapes imaginable. They are a pure shining white. Some appear as if they were built by man and have square edges. Others look like clusters of huge candles dripping wax. Caves and niches are gouged in them. Some are capped with strange toppings that look like hats. I have made some pictures because the shapes are so peculiar. The river twists and turns and runs level through this country.

We are sore from pulling the canoes. The river made a turn from north northwest to south southwest today. The mountains look no closer. When will this river end?

June 3, 1805

Another large river joins us here. We have made camp at the point of connection. It sets a problem for us. Which river is truly the Missouri? The Hidatsas told us that the Missouri runs deep into the western mountains and then it is half a day's portage over these to the place where a new river called the Columbia begins and slides down to the sea. I accompanied both Captains, who hiked to a high bluff to see if they could solve this problem and see which river to follow. This new river comes from the north. The Hidatsa had said nothing about it. However, the Indians had spoken of some great falls to which the Missouri led, and after the falls was a place where indeed the rivers of this huge country divide. The Captains are calling it the Continental Divide. All the rivers east of the divide flow east, while those west, like the Columbia, flow west. The Captains are really stumped because this river that seems to come from the north looks a lot more like the water and the currents of the Missouri, which we have traveled on all these long months, while the water of the south fork is much clearer and more tranquil in its movement.

They returned to camp to ask Sacajawea's opinion, but she said she does not know, for we are not yet near her country.

June 4, 1805

The Captains are still undecided. Captain Lewis will set out on an exploration of the north fork, and Captain Clark the Southern. I am to accompany Captain Lewis along with some of the other men. They hope to be able to figure out which is the true Missouri. We made good miles on foot. Close to thirty today.

June 7, 1805

It has begun to rain. We keep walking and are still no closer to figuring out which river to follow.

Later: Had a terrible fright this afternoon. The mud had become as slick as grease, and we were edging our way along a narrow cliff trail when suddenly Captain Lewis's feet went out from under him and he was hanging off the edge of the cliff. He wrenched himself back up onto the edge and to safety, but not one minute later, we heard another cry. Private Windsor had slipped over the same cliff edge. Windsor was hanging there shaking like a leaf in the breeze, and I expected to see him plummet three hundred feet to the rocks below, but the Captain, his voice as steady as could be, softly says, "Take out your knife, Private, and commence to dig a hole for your foot. In that way you shall gain a hold." Windsor did as he was told and was soon back on the top again. We all go now like snails.

Captain Lewis has decided to name this confounding river that comes from the north Maria's River. He hasn't said but I am guessing that Maria is the Captain's sweetheart. So now each of the Captains' sweethearts has a river named for her. That's more than most women get in this life.

June 9, 1805

We returned to camp last night. Both Captains are convinced that the true Missouri is that which branches south. But not one man in the Corps including myself believes them. We all feel they are wrong. And yet, every man in the Corps, myself included, shall follow our Captains. The two men are so determined in their beliefs that I think we all feel it would be most disrespectful not to follow them. So we start tomorrow, for it is late in the season and there is not a minute to be wasted. The Hidatsa told us that snows can come as early as September. And although every man thinks we are headed up the wrong river, we are all still a contented lot, and tonight Cruzatte got out his fiddle and played us several merry tunes.

June 11, 1805

Captain Lewis has been sick with dysentery. He asks that I fetch the Glauber's salts and mix up a decoction from the chokecherries he has picked.

June 13, 1805

I was walking with Captain Lewis today when both of us at the same time heard an odd whining in our ears. "The falls!" Captain Lewis exclaimed. Indeed the Captains had made the right choice to follow the south fork of the rivers, for this was the true Missouri and as the Hidatsas had said, it led to some great falls. Very soon the whine became a roar. We were both so excited that when we returned to camp we could hardly speak fast enough. We had a delicious feast to celebrate tonight—buffalo hump, beaver tail, trout, buffalo tongue, and the marrow from their bones.

June 14, 1805

Today Captain Lewis and several of us set out for the falls. The spray billowed up like smoke, but as we drew closer we saw a single bright white sheet of water that fell over the edge. This first ledge of the falls is some two hundred yards wide, but there are falls beyond this and then more and more falls. We think there might be as many as five or six. We walked on to the second rank of falls. They are huge and powerful. They flash with light and spin rainbows in their crashing descent into the frothing waters below.

June 16, 1805

I barely have time to write for myself because Captain Lewis has kept me busy all day copying his journals. We have discovered that there are indeed five separate falls, all of them huge and mighty. We have set our camp at the base of the first one. It is going to be a long portage.

Later: Captain Clark just appeared in the tent where Captain Lewis and I have been transcribing notes to tell us that Sacajawea is very ill. They gave her some opium and a decoction made of the special bark Captain Lewis often uses for poultices. The Captain has asked me to fetch some water from a sulfur spring we came across on one of our walks on the riverbanks. He thinks the sulfur in the water might do her some good. They have bled her twice.

June 17, 1805

I stayed up with Sacajawea and the Captain all night as he treated her. I couldn't do much to help her, but I held Pomp and tried to rock him and keep him happy. Come dawn this morning her pulse began to grow stronger and more regular. Captain Lewis feels this is a very good sign.

June 21, 1805

After much exploring in the region of the falls our portage around them begins today. The canoes are mounted on sleds with wheels and we must pull. If the wind backs around behind us we shall hoist their sails to ease our hauling. It will be an eighteen-mile portage. The Captains at first thought it would be just half a day, but now they are saying at least three. They divided the party in two. I shall go with Captain Clark, Sacajawea, Charbonneau, York, and a couple of other men.

June 25, 1805

This is the hardest thing I have ever had to do in my life. I have never been so tired. Every bone in my body aches. We must haul these canoes and all the gear over hills and rocky knobs that are perhaps not quite hills, too big to go around but not small enough to get over easily. Tall grass reaches out to snag us. There is mud to slip on and steep gullies. We limp, our feet are sore, our backs ache. Captain Clark directs the portage. Captain Lewis has stayed behind working on his "experiment." The experiment is an iron-frame boat for descending the Columbia. They have brought the pieces all the way from St. Louis, and they hope to assemble the rods of iron and then stretch hide over it. Everyone except Captain Lewis doubts it shall work. There is no telling Captain Lewis it won't work.

June 28, 1805

The portage continues. Too tired to write. Feet blistered. Bad sore on shoulder from pulling rope. Windsor fainted today. I have a prickly pear needle festering in my heel. We had rain. The temperature dropped suddenly and hail as big as apples was beating down on us. We are on the eighth day of what was supposed to be a three-day portage. Our moccasins last no more than two days. We have learned to sew them real good using double soles of parfleche and buffalo hide.

June 29, 1805

We nearly met our end today. We were about a quarter of a mile above the falls when it started to rain. It just came pounding down and then a sudden squall chased in. We all ran for a rock shelter above the falls that was in a deep ravine. York had raced ahead and found it. There was some rock shelf sticking out for protection—or so we thought. We all huddled there, and wouldn't you know it, Charbonneau found the driest spot under the overhang. I was trying to inch my way over and draw Sacajawea and Pomp in closer when suddenly it was as if a wall of water came tearing down the ravine carrying mud and rock and more water than you could ever imagine. I yanked Sacajawea back and Pomp and the hide pack cradle in which she carries the baby with her came off into my arms. Then I don't know what happened but I felt the pack just slip away. I saw it skid off on a slab of sliding mud. Pomp screamed and I dived across for him, and by some miracle I grabbed hold of his little shoulders. The cradle board went cascading down with slides of mud and rock and Sacajawea screamed. I've never heard such a scream in my life. It was almost as if you could not just hear it but see it, like a bolt of lightning torn from her throat. She started to dive headlong because she thought Pomp was falling into the ravine, but Captain Clark reached out and grabbed her and spun her around and she saw

Pomp squashed into my arms. She just collapsed, shaking on the ground with relief. And Charbonneau didn't say a word. He sat as dry as could be in his corner. But York gave him such a look as to freeze his blood. Pomp lost all his swaddling blankets. And I guess I pulled him right out of his little breeches. I am going to help Sacajawea start sewing some new clothes for him tonight.

July 1, 1805

We have seen grizzlies almost every day but I think we look so miserably skinny and tough and genuinely poor that they have no interest in chomping into us. They'd probably spit us out after the first bite.

July 2, 1805

Portage is finished. We rest here for several days before getting on the river again.

July 3, 1805

Captain Lewis keeps fiddling with the iron-frame boat that they brought up here. It's leaking like a fishnet. Even Captain Clark thinks this is a folly. He says nothing but I can tell what he is thinking nonetheless.

July 4, 1805

It is the United States of America's twenty-ninth birthday today. The Captains gave us all a gill of whiskey. It burned so with the first swallow, I gave the rest to Joe Field. Good supper: beans and bacon, dumplings, buffalo hump.

July 6, 1805

My heel where the prickly pear needle went in is still bothering me. I thought I got it all out.

Later: Sacajawea took a look at my foot and came back within a few minutes with a bag full of thimbleberry leaves. She steeped them in hot water and then wrapped my heel in them. She did this three more times this evening. My heel is feeling better. The redness is gone.

July 9, 1805

Captain Lewis has given up on the iron-frame boat. Never thought I'd see this man give up on anything. But the hide began to separate at the seams in spite of all the work. Good Lord, he caulked those seams with every thing from tallow to pine gum. We were counting on the iron-frame boat for hauling equipment. Now short one boat, we're delayed while we get to work making two new canoes.

I wanted to get out of here sooner, as the mosquitoes are something fierce. I know Sacajawea is anxious, too, for soon she will be coming into her home territory.

July 15, 1805

We set out today. The mountains look a little bit closer and a lot bigger. I learn these mountains are called the Rockies. So far we have just called them the mountains. But more and more I hear the Captains speak of them as the Rockies. I sense that they are nothing like the gentle red soil and grassy low mountains of Virginia with which both the Captains are so familiar.

July 17, 1805

Everyone is most anxious to meet up with the Shoshoni. We keep a sharp eye out for signs. The Captains are talking about sending out a party under Clark to scout for them.

July 19, 1805

Hard morning on the river. The river narrows and grows shallower. We had to use the ropes for dragging as well as the setting poles. But none of that was as tough as when we rounded a bend, and then we saw them. The Rockies broke through—immense, high peaks jagged and crusted with snow. This ain't Virginia, and my heart sank down to my moccasins.

Later: We passed through cliffs on the other side of the river late this afternoon. They rise more than a thousand feet into the air. Captain Lewis calls them the gates of the Rocky Mountains. I feel pressed in between these cliffs and the wall of mountains ahead. It is like a stone coffin.

July 20, 1805

We pass now through a wide fertile valley, and for this brief day the immense mountains did not seem to close in on us with their lofty peaks. Captain Clark has set out with a scouting party to look for Shoshoni. I cannot understand why he did not take Sacajawea with him. He did ask her the word for "white man" so that if he encounters the Shoshoni he might explain who we are. The word she told him is *tab-ba-bone*. She explained to me that the word "white man" is hard to translate and that this word really means "stranger." I think they should have taken her with them. I think they feel they need her only to get them horses but not to introduce them and explain their mission.

July 22, 1805
Shoshoni country

Hurrah! Suddenly this afternoon, as if mists had cleared from her eyes, Sacajawea recognized that we were entering her home territory. She nearly danced down the river, recognizing trees and boulders and bends. The going was very tough today. Our shoulders are tired from hauling the canoes through shallow water. The way along shore is not much better, as there is a most fiercesome grass that grows in this region. We are calling it needle grass because it has barbed seeds that stab through our moccasins and tear at our skin. But the knowledge that Sacajawea now surely knows the way lightens us all.

We met up with Captain Clark. He has seen no Indians and plans to set off tomorrow in search once more. And once more he refuses to take Sacajawea.

July 28, 1805

We have come to a point in the river where three forks meet. Captain Clark had arrived two days before. There is a southeast, a southwest, and a middle fork. Captain Lewis has named them the Jefferson, for our President, the Madison, in honor of James Madison, the secretary of state, and the Gallatin, for the secretary of treasury. We go on naming this land, but I wonder if the world that reads this map that Captain Clark is making will ever know what Sacajawea told me this evening—that this is near the very spot where her mother was murdered by the Minnetarees and where she herself was kidnapped. She pointed in the direction of a creek where her best friend from childhood, who was also captured, had jumped across to escape the Minnetarees when they had briefly turned the other way. Sacajawea also said something that really surprised me. Her name before she was captured was not Sacajawea but Bo-i-nav, which means Grass Girl. There is a lot of thick, tall grass around here. She told me that because of their horse herds they always looked for grass so the horses could graze, and that when she was a little girl she once got lost in the tall grass but that she found her way back to the camp all by herself. So they named her Grass Girl.

This spot where we now are, where she was captured, will probably be known only as a place named for great men and never for Sacajawea or her friend who had courage equal to any president, I think, or any secretary of the state or treasury.

August 1, 1805

I can tell that Captain Lewis is anxious because we have not yet seen any Shoshoni. The summer is quickly passing to fall and the fall to winter. We must have horses to help us across the mountains.

August 3, 1805

Sacajawea has told Captain Lewis how we passed near the spot where she was captured some years ago. I did not know she had told him until I was working with him in his tent tonight on various specimens and the journals. He asked that I make copies of some entries. I was shocked when I read his words about her capture. He wrote, "I cannot discover that she shows any emotion of sorrow in recollecting this event . . . or any joy in being again restored to her native country; if she has enough to eat and a few trinkets to wear I believe she would be perfectly content anywhere." I think Captain Lewis is absolutely wrong. Just because she never shows her feelings does not mean she hasn't any. And as for trinkets, well, Sacajawea told me herself that the one "trinket" she would most love to own is the Captain's sextant and quadrant by which she would like to learn to mark the position of the stars in the sky and her own place on earth. She couldn't care less for beads — even blue ones.

August 8, 1805

We all took great cheer today as we rounded a bend in the Jefferson River and Sacajawea cried for joy (I hope Captain Lewis remarked on this display of emotion), for she recognized the hill that rears like the head of a beaver. She says we are very close now to the summer campgrounds of her people. This indeed lifted everyone's spirits.

August 10, 1805

Captain Lewis spotted an Indian today. He shouted, "Tab-ba-bone," and by gum if that Indian didn't turn and run. Captain Lewis is very upset.

We are approaching the divide of the continent now, and from there we shall see what road lies ahead. I believe that the Captains honestly think that the Columbia River will start almost as soon as the Missouri ends, or perhaps they think it shall begin after a short portage to the top of the mountains and then those mountains will sweep down gently to the west.

August 12, 1805
The Great Divide

Today in the early morning we were most of us hiking. The river indeed had narrowed to a stream and had broken off into small rivulets. We began to climb a small slope. Then at about ten this morning Joe Field, Hugh McNeal, and I stood with each of our feet on either side of the most central rivulet. McNeal exclaimed, "This is it, boys! We done got here. This river has ended!" We were at the headwaters of the Missouri—at last.

Then we continued on, following Captain Lewis and others as we climbed toward the top of the ridge before us. We would be the first from the new American nation to look beyond this ridge that divides the rivers of the continent and look to the northwest. At the top of the pass I must tell you I felt the dream, President Jefferson's dream of a water route to the western ocean, running out like sand in an hourglass. I look around at the faces of the men and I think I am seeing the dream run out right there.

One cannot imagine our shock, for we saw not another river tumbling down to the west and to the shores of a distant sea. No! We saw more mountains, high and higher, and beyond them other ranges—range upon range, snow covered and with no hope of a river through them. The river has ended but these mountains are as high as the stars, and they are waiting for us. We left most of our party on the eastern side of the pass over the dividing ridge with most of the baggage.

Captain Lewis, Drouillard, and eight of us descended the western slope of the divide and made camp. The long shadows of the huge mountains in the setting sun stretched out, turning the evening light purple. An odd silence came upon us tonight. No one spoke much. Not one word was said about the Rockies.

August 13, 1805

This morning Captain Lewis and Drouillard and I set off early before first light. The Captain is fixed on meeting an Indian. Sure enough, after walking almost ten miles we see three Indian women. The Captain starts calling out, "Tab-ba-bone." I felt like a dang fool because then he said I should start shouting this, too. I mean, I think we both must have looked like idiots, walking in this high country, yelling this word that doesn't quite mean what it is supposed to. How would we feel if two Indians came walking down a street back in a place like St. Louis shouting, "Red Stranger! Red Stranger!" He managed to speak to them in sign language with Drouillard's help. We gave them some beads and vermillion paint for their cheeks and then asked the women to take a message to their chiefs. Then finally, not more than an hour later, we saw an entire party, at least fifty Shoshoni coming toward us. I got to admire the Captain, for even though they looked like a war party, he quickly laid down his rifle.

This was our first meeting. It went well. Everyone sat

down to parley. The pipe was brought out. The Shoshoni took off their moccasins. Sacajawea had told us this was a sign of friendship. The chief's name is Cameahwait. I wish Sacajawea had been there with us. I think it's not fit that I should see her people before she does, and Captain Lewis should feel rotten about this, but he doesn't. I honestly think he believes what he writes about Sacajawea having few feelings. In any case Sacajawea and Charbonneau are accompanying Captain Clark on a several days' exploration of the Jefferson River.

August 14, 1805

We accompanied Cameahwait to their village this evening. They are wretchedly poor. They offered us a piece of salmon and some awful-tasting boiled root. Although they are very poor they are rich in horses. I would guess from just looking about that they have several hundred. Cameahwait and the Captain talk more. The chief and his people want guns. If they have guns, they say, they will be able to shoot buffalo and not have to eat so much of these bitter roots, which nourish them little. The Captain asked Cameahwait to cross back over the divide with him in the morning, and to bring thirty horses or more with him. They will meet up with Clark and the rest of the party on the eastern side of the pass at the forks of the Jefferson.

August 16, 1805

We crossed back over the pass. The Captain calls it Lemhi Pass now since the Shoshoni told him it is a passage to Lemhi River. We made our camp near a creek. Drouillard went out hunting and came back with a deer. The Indians were so starved they could hardly wait. They had heard the shot and met up with Drouillard at the kill site. When I arrived I saw a gruesome feast. They had not waited to start a fire or even do proper butchering. Blood ran down the Shoshoni warriors' faces as they scooped out the kidneys and the liver and tore hunks of meat off the deer, eating it raw! But I was soon moved to pity, as I have never seen such poor starving creatures in all my life.

August 17, 1805

Captain Clark arrived at our camp this morning with Sacajawea. Just as Sacajawea was coming up I heard one of the warrior's women make a little squealing sound. Then it was as if a whirlwind whipped by me and she sprang toward Sacajawea, who cried out and sprang toward her. The two began embracing each other and rubbing cheeks together and hugging and crying. Sacajawea turned to me and stuck her fingers in her mouth and made loud sucking noises, then crossed her arms over her chest. Through a dance of gestures I soon realized that this was her best friend from childhood, the one who had been captured with her and escaped. Her name is now Jumping Fish, for she had sprung, much as she had today, across the stream to escape the Hidatsas. And then there was more commotion. I had noticed as Sacajawea and Jumping Fish settled down into a quiet stream of tears of joy that Sacajawea had begun to stare at Cameahwait. Suddenly she raced across the bare ground, and running toward him, threw her blanket over him, a sign for blood relation. The chief Cameahwait is her brother! Her tears did not stop the whole morning. I doubt that Captain Lewis shall ever write in his journals again that Sacajawea shows no emotion or any joy in being restored to her native country. And certainly trinkets and a full belly are not enough to fill her soul and make her content. Because of the happy events that happened here the Captains have named this place Camp Fortunate.

August 18, 1805

Today is Captain Lewis's thirty-first birthday. He seems happy. He should be, as Cameahwait has gone back to his village to fetch more horses and mules to help transport us across this Lemhi Pass and hopefully over the immense mountains beyond. Some of our baggage we shall leave behind buried or hidden. The canoes will be left for there is no water route through those mountains. You'd have to be as dumb as a chicken to haul those canoes up the Rockies. When we get across and down to the Columbia we shall build new ones.

I forgot to mention that I noticed that Sacajawea when she arrived in camp yesterday had a big bruise along the right side of her face. I asked her about it and she kind of shrugged, but then she told me that Charbonneau got mad at her and hit her. Lucky for her it was right when Captain Clark was walking up. The Captain got so mad that he picked up Charbonneau and threw him into a patch of thorns.

August 22, 1805

Cameahwait arrived back in camp today along with Sacajawea and Charbonneau, who had gone with him back to the village. We shall begin our portage across the pass in a day or so. Captain Clark gave Charbonneau money to buy a horse for Sacajawea.

August 25, 1805

Bad news. Charbonneau overheard that Cameahwait plans to leave us high and dry halfway up the Lemhi Pass, where we are now, and go off and hunt buffalo with another band of Shoshoni. Captain Lewis is fit to be tied. I have never seen him so mad. He gave Charbonneau a tongue blistering the likes of which I never heard. I guess Charbonneau has known about this plan for a while and never said a word to the Captain till after noon. A meeting was called. Sacajawea was there. I knew judging by the length at which she spoke that she was saying more than just the words Captain Lewis had said. She was truly convincing her brother that this was a dishonorable thing to do — to go back on his word. I guess she convinced him, because we are going forward again tomorrow.

August 26, 1805

We have crossed over the pass and now make our camp on the river called Lemhi. It is freezing cold. The Captain ordered Cruzatte to play the fiddle and the men to dance. But I can tell that the Captain is wary. He is still fearful that the Shoshoni will not make good on their promise of horses.

August 27, 1805

I had been thinking that Sacajawea was unusually quiet since returning from the Shoshoni village. Finally tonight she told me. She said that the man she was supposed to have married, who had been picked out by her family, had come up when she got there and claimed her as his wife. But when he found out she had had a child by Charbonneau, he no longer wanted her. I had never fully realized until that moment that Sacajawea had probably planned to stay in her village, if not right then, at least afterward when the Corps comes back east from the western ocean. She had planned to leave that lout Charbonneau, but now she can't. But then she said maybe it was for the better. This I didn't understand, but she explained that the man she was supposed to marry was an ugly old fellow and, besides that, many of the women of her village look hard on her now that she has a horse to ride, for indeed Captain Clark gave her one of the horses they got from the Shoshoni. Women do not have their own horses to ride among the Shoshoni and this sets her above her kind. So here she is, stuck again somewhere between nations, and like that badger, forever caught between worlds, not quite alive and not quite dead.

August 29, 1805

Captain Lewis was right to worry about the horses. Cameahwait just raised the price for the rest of the horses. Captain Clark had to throw in a pistol, a knife, and one hundred rounds of ammunition. The Captains broke one of their own rules: never to cut down on their own store of weapons and ammunition. But those mountains are high and those horses will prove better protection than guns. I think those Shoshoni don't need any lessons in Yankee trading. They're the best dang traders I ever seen. I think Sacajawea was pretty happy to see the price go up, to tell you the truth. She said that when she went back with her brother to his village, she could scarcely believe how poor they were.

September 2, 1805
The Bitterroots

We moved down from the Lemhi River two days ago and follow the north fork of Fish Creek. The way is steep and slippery. Many of the horses have fallen and today we made only five miles. Nearly all of the Shoshoni except for an old man the Captains call Old Toby and his sons have turned back. There is no trail, no sign of a living person, Indian or white. But there are the mountains ahead. Their shadows begin to reach out for us soon after midday. With each step the way climbs higher.

September 3, 1805

Woke up to snow this morning. It comes down steadily all day. Our last thermometer broke. I have worry deep in my gut and not much of anything else, because we ate the last of the salt pork two days ago. Game is scarce here. Our route is nearly due north. We travel with the divide to our right.

September 5, 1805

Hard freeze last night. Came to a north-flowing river yesterday that we have named the Clark River. So now the Captains and their sweethearts all have rivers. This afternoon we met up with some Indians that the Shoshoni call the Salish, but the Captains call them the Flatheads. That is what they are calling all these northwest Indians — Flatheads because they heard that many of the tribes in this section of the country have a way of pressing their babies' heads with a board when they are in the cradle to make the foreheads flat and the crown of their heads rise up. I cannot imagine it myself, and so far we have not seen any real flat heads. So I'll just call these Indians the Salish. They seem very friendly. Old Toby is most helpful in talking to them as is Sacajawea, because their language is close to that of the Salish.

September 11, 1805

Weather bad. The snow is heavy and wet. I carry Pomp in the hide carrier for a while. Although Sacajawea rides on a horse, Pomp is still a heavy load. He is seven months old now and weighs close to twenty pounds, and when his diapers are soaking, which is most of the time, I am sure he weighs more than twenty.

September 13, 1805

We are almost always cold and hungry. Very hungry. We now eat only the awful portable soup. It fills you up for about five minutes but then you are hungrier than before.

September 14, 1805

We were so hungry today that we were forced to kill one of the young colts to eat. We call our campsite tonight on the south fork of this creek Colt Killed Creek.

September 16, 1805

I was on guard duty tonight. It began snowing, snowing hard three hours before daybreak. This does not look good.

Later: I think this is maybe the worst day of the entire expedition. We are all so cold and hungry and low in spirits. The horses are starving. The Captains ordered another horse killed to feed us. We are well into these mountains that some of the Indians call the Bitterroot because of that foul-tasting root the Shoshoni fed us when we first met them. Nothing else seems to grow here, except big trees, and you can't eat them. Game is scarce and we name this country after the horses we kill to eat. The dream died when we crossed the divide and saw only mountains ahead, no water route. Now we live the nightmare.

September 17, 1805

We eat bear grease. Sacajawea scoops handfuls of snow to keep her thin milk from drying up completely. I learned a new word from Sacajawea. *Puha*. It means courage. She cuts me a patch of mountain sheep hide and tells me to rub my face with it many times a day. It will prevent frostbite.

September 19, 1805

Captain Clark, who moves in advance of us, killed a stray horse and left it hanging in a tree for us. We set upon it instantly. The horse meat was tough but flavorful. Sacajawea chewed small pieces until they were like paste and then spit them out and gave them to Pomp, who made a sweet little sound—"ummmmuhummmuh"—as if he were enjoying every bite, or I guess every lick, for he has only one tooth.

If there is a stray horse in this region we must be coming close to the settlements. These are Indians that Old Toby calls the Pierced Noses. Francis says the French trappers all call them the Nez Percé, which means the same. It is hard for me to believe any human could live in these mountains.

September 21, 1805

Reuben Field, who had gone with Captain Clark, came back and told us that today they came upon two villages of the Nez Percé.

September 23, 1805

We have caught up with Clark at the second village of the Nez Percé. The chief here is a tall old man named Twisted Hair. We are the first white people these Indians have ever seen. They treat us with great respect, and they make us cakes of camas roots and feed us dried salmon. Captain Clark tells us not to overeat as we have been on short rations for so long we shall get sick with the dysentery.

September 24, 1805

Except for Sacajawea and Pomp we are all sick as dogs with dysentery. I don't think the Field brothers are as sick as the rest of us, for they make terrible and crude jokes about us all running into the trees. Some are fairly funny but Father Dumaine would not want me to repeat them here. Well, one has to do with us making a new Missouri River that's even muddier! Yes, very crude. My stomach cramps something fierce. Must run!

September 25, 1805

Still sick. Captain Lewis gave me some of Dr. Rush's pills, not the Thunderclappers, and a dose of jalap salts.

September 26, 1805

Those who are well enough begin to make canoes. Twisted Hair says that the creek by which we camp flows into one called the Clearwater, which is then joined by another river from the northeast and flows west into the Columbia. He says it is five sleeps, no more, to the Columbia River from here and then another five sleeps to the falls of the Columbia. It is probably ten. Whenever anyone tells us that something is one distance I just plain double it.

The Captains handed out medals and beads and gave the Big Speech and all the usual. In return we received dried roots, berries, and dried fish.

October 2, 1805

We make good progress on building the canoes. Twisted Hair showed us how to burn out the center of the big logs. This is good and it makes short work of what would take weeks. Within one day we have a canoe in the rough. Many are still plagued with the dysentery, but not Sacajawea. I think she is used to this food—the camas roots and dried fish.

October 5, 1805

The canoes are finished. I help the Captains cache some paddles and canisters of powder and other equipment for the trip back east. Both Captains are feeling poorly and have troubles with their stomach and bowels. I don't for the moment. Thank goodness.

October 7, 1805

Sick or not we put those canoes in the water by three o'clock this afternoon and are going downstream of the

Clearwater. The Indian name for this river is the Kŏs Kŏs Kee. It runs very rapidly and has shoal swift places. But it sure does feel good to go downstream instead of up for the first time ever on this journey. Old Toby and his two sons are still with us, and Twisted Hair has agreed to come along, too, for he knows some of the Indians in these parts.

October 9, 1805

We hit some fairly scarifying rapids today. They boiled up high and furious. The Captains didn't want to lose time with a portage around them. So we ran them. God must have been looking out for us. I don't know how else we could have done it but we got through them safe. However, our guide Old Toby and his sons took off this evening not even waiting for their pay. I think they thought, Enough of these crazy white folks. We're getting out of here before they really get us killed!

October 10, 1805

We reached the Snake River today. We must be closing in on the Columbia. We are so sick of eating dried fish. Some of the men bought dogs from Indians around here and have been eating them. But not me.

October 14, 1805

Thank heavens, Captain Clark shot some ducks today. I was pretty excited, but I swear I bit into that first hunk of duck and dang if it didn't have a fishy taste! I think everything eats fish out here.

The Indians in these parts are friendly, but I think a lot has to do with the Captains sending Sacajawea ahead with Twisted Hair. Captain Clark says when you send a woman out ahead, the Indians know that this ain't no war party, but that we're interested in peace. Captain Lewis is interested in words. He has this list of words, and Sacajawea is supposed to find out the Indian word for each one. Of course she doesn't know how to read or write so she has to keep the list in her head. It is amazing how she can keep a list of forty or fifty words in her head. When I am with her I have the list written down. It has words like fish, fur, bear, eagle, canoe, moccasins. Common words. The words differ from tribe to tribe but not that much. There are a mess of different tribes in the region of the Snake and the Columbia Rivers—the Nez Percé, of course, also called the Cho-pun-nish around here, then the Yakama, the Wanapams, the Walla Walla, then farther along the Chinooks. The Cho-pun-nish dress in otter skins and for jewelry hang many beautiful shells from their ears and braid them into their hair as well. Mother-of-pearl is one of their favorites for decoration.

The men don't wear much below the waist. They don't seem to care who sees what. The women are more modest and wear the skins of big-horn goats worked into shirts or long tunics, which they decorate with more shells, beads, and porcupine quills.

October 15, 1805

Took a walk with Captain Lewis this evening on a high plain above the river. In the far, far distance we saw a mountain range. These are the mountains of the Pacific.

October 16, 1805
Columbia River

We are now at the junction of the Snake and Columbia Rivers. The Captain had a meeting with the head chief in this region. They sent me to get the medals and now some handkerchiefs, as we have no blue beads left. I've never seen an Indian blow his nose on a piece of cloth so I sure don't know what they'll make of these handkerchiefs. We got some dried fish and dried horse meat in exchange. Captain Lewis had me working on the word lists again. The whole country around here stinks because many of the streams and parts of the river are choked up with dead salmon. The salmon swim upstream to lay their eggs every year. Then they die right afterward. I'd die, too, if I had to swim buck naked up these streams. You should see these fish. They're all bashed up and bloody. I can't help but wonder how they even get the strength to lay their eggs once they get here.

October 17, 1805

The Indians are very friendly. They come out on the river-banks as we pass. They offer us dried fish and dog meat. I still have not eaten dog meat and don't intend to either. The women dress differently here than upstream. They are not nearly so modest and wear only a small piece of leather around their hips and drawn between their legs. Maybe this is because the women work right alongside the men and must be ready to hop in and out of canoes and carry them on their backs or wade into the river with their fish baskets. I even saw one woman chopping down a large tree by herself. We were invited into one village and into the lodge of one family. I noticed that in the corner was a very, very old woman. She sat on a pile of rich otter furs and a young child was gently feeding her a bit of salmon. Another young girl was combing her hair, and another on the other side was braiding in pretty shells. We were told that this woman had lived more than one hundred winters and that she is blind. We asked if she was the mother or grandmother of a great chief and they said no. We understand now that she is treated this way simply because she is so old. The people who call themselves in this region the Chin-na-pum value her because she is so old and has seen so many winters. This is very different from many tribes.

Sacajawea told me that the Shoshoni and the Minnetaree leave their old people to die alone on the plains or in the mountains. She told me that when her own grandmother became so old she could no longer walk, they built her a shelter and left her with only some water and pemmican. I guess this is the difference of being old in a tribe that must always move. The Shoshoni must always follow the horse herds for grazing. The Minnetarees and the Hidatsa travel over far ranges for hunting, but these people, the Chin-na-pum, stay mostly here on the banks of the river. It is therefore, I suppose, on the banks of a river that one does not have to fear growing old. It is on the banks of a river that your great-great-grandchildren will think your wrinkles are beautiful and braid mother-of-pearl into your hair.

October 23, 1805

We now come to the most dangerous part of the river with many falls and rapids too many to count. We make an exploration trip on foot several miles down. Sometimes the river narrows between high cliffs and the water pours through in gigantic churning rushes. The sound roars and one's own voice cannot be heard above it. But the Captains have decided that there is only one place where the river drops twenty feet or more that will have to be portaged. They figure that the rest we can pass through. I am not so sure. We see the Indians of these parts do it, but they are expert watermen and their canoes are the best we have seen so far. Beautifully made and light, they seem to skim through the most turbulent water. Each canoe has an animal carved on its bow. Our canoes look ugly and awkward by comparison. These Indians who make the good canoes are called Chinooks.

October 24, 1805

We did make it. I am not sure how we did it through the first set of falls. But what awaits us today is worse. The Captains have decided to send by land all those who cannot swim and they shall carry the scientific equipment, all the journals, and the other valuable articles. The canoes are simply too heavy for this portage, so they must go with those of us who can swim. That's me, among others. I wish it weren't. I look down into this swelling, boiling water and I think I'm going to wind up looking like one of those bashed-up salmon. Even the Indians can't believe we're going to try this. There are more than a hundred of them along the banks just watching for these stupid white men to go down the river. This might be the funniest thing they've seen in years.

October 25, 1805

I'm alive. Just barely. I surely don't know why, but we made it. More falls to come. Still time to die.

November 3, 1805

I have never been so happy to be through with anything in my life as with those cascading falls of the Columbia River. It would be hard to say which is worse, freezing and starving to death in the Bitterroot Mountains or being mashed up in the Columbia River, but somehow we did it. The worst came at the end with the Great Chute. Here indeed we had to portage the canoes and the baggage, although at places using elk skin ropes and manning them from the banks, we could run the canoes through without men in them.

We are now camped on an island. The fog is so thick I can't see Seaman, who just rushed off and is no more than twenty feet from me. I can hear him snuffing around. Then out of the fog I hear Pomp laugh. Seaman must be licking him. He loves it when Seaman does this.

Later: You know who stood up in that fog and took a step, holding on to Seaman? Pomp!! Never heard of a boy walking so young. Not quite talking but I bet he will be by Christmas.

November 4, 1805

Been raining every day in this country, and fog hangs in the air most of the time. But we make at least thirty miles each day. The Indians are very poor looking and dirty, and we must keep a sharp watch at night, for many things are disappearing. We did see our first big canoes that the Captains say are the coastal ones from the sea. The largest one has a bear head carved on it. Very handsome.

November 7, 1805

The fog really cleared off today and suddenly Captain Clark stood up and then shouted so as to shake the entire canoe. "The ocean! The ocean is in view!" We were all so excited that every canoe began to rock as men forgot and began to stand up and dance and jump. My Lord, after all these miles, after 4,124 miles to be exact, to see the ocean! We quickly went to the bank of the river and the Captains sent me up a tree. I crawled out on a long branch that pointed west and yes, even as it began to rain I could see it. It was a blue smear, like a distant frayed ribbon pressed beneath the heavy gray sky. The great Pacific Ocean.

November 8, 1805

As we proceed we feel the great pull of the ocean's tide even though we are several miles from it. We must regard the ebb and the flow of the tide and make our camp with this in mind. The water is already very salty to the taste and gains salt with each mile.

November 10, 1805

The weather is terrible and has been for two days. Lashed by heavy winds and rains. Trees are uprooted and the river throws up huge waves. Everything is wet and cold. This is a terrible campsite for we seem to catch every wind and torrent of foul weather. There is no shelter in this bay of the river. The food is all bad, for most of our meat has spoiled and many of the men are feeling very ill. One might think our main purpose for being here is to feed the fleas. They have found us and invaded—our hair, our clothes, every part of our body. There is talk of looking for another campsite, for indeed we shall have to spend the winter here before we begin our homeward journey.

November 13, 1805

I am to leave within the hour with Shannon and Privates John Colter and Willard and Reuben and Joseph Field to explore the river and around the point for another campsite. We will take two canoes.

November 14, 1805

Last night we found a better campsite on a sandy beach in the bay. Colter and Reuben Field returned to tell the Captains. I was glad I was not expected to go for I did something else. This morning before daybreak I left our camp alone and made my way toward the sea. I am the first person of this expedition to stand at the edge of the western ocean. Its water has touched my moccasins. But this sea was not shining for it was dawn and the sun was still rising in the east and had not touched it yet. Nor was it Pacific and peaceful as its name says. The waves rolled in with thunderous roars.

But now this evening I come once more and watch as the sun sets, and for the time the rain has stopped. The waves still crash but when I look out beyond the froth of the breaking water, I do indeed see a shining sea, spilling now with such colors. It is as if a rainbow of water has been laid down and stretches forever. I think back. I began this journal with my ear just stitched up with wildcat gut after it nearly got sliced off. I go back to that first page of this journal and I can see the drop of blood, faded but still there. I cannot believe how far I have come. I have crossed mountains and paddled long rivers. I have held a baby and made a friend named Bird Woman. I have learned how to find my true place standing on earth using the stars. I have named a falls Silverwing Woman that runs with silver cords of water, and now I have come to the Shining Sea. I bend down and take some drops of this water. You ever see ink mixed with salt water?

Epilogue

Augustus Pelletier never forgot the Shining Sea. He returned with the Lewis and Clark expedition which arrived in St. Louis on September 23, 1806. He continued to assist Meriwether Lewis with the organization of his notes, journals, and various specimens even after Captain Lewis had been appointed governor of the Louisiana territory. Lewis however fell into a deep depression and committed suicide on October 11, 1809. At that time Captain William Clark turned his and Lewis's journals over to Nicholas Biddle, a Philadelphia lawyer, to edit. He recommended that Biddle hire Augustus Pelletier, who was the person most familiar with Lewis's notes and specimens. Augustus worked for a time with Biddle but then became frustrated with the slow pace of the work. He longed to see the Shining Sea again. At the age of twenty he hired himself out as a guide for the Missouri Fur Trading company. He soon became known as a good fur trader and at the mouth of the Columbia river opened a trading station that served American ships purchasing furs from the China trade which was just beginning.

Augustus was very successful yet there was great unrest among the Indians. On a trip back east to explore the possibilities of opening an office in St. Louis for his fur trading he saw Sacajawea. She had remained for a time in Saint Louis, with her son Jean Baptiste, at the home of Captain William Clark, who had married his sweetheart, Judith. She then joined Charbonneau on the upper Missouri where he spent the rest of his life interpreting for government officials. They did however leave their son Jean Baptiste behind with the Clark family to be educated. In 1812 Sacajawea gave birth to a second child, a daughter Lisette, at Fort Mandan but later that winter Sacajawea fell ill and died.

When Augustus learned of Sacajawea's death he was deeply saddened. Captain Clark had promised to educate Sacajawea's children and it was Augustus who helped arrange for the tiny child Lisette to be returned to St. Louis. He visited the children regularly over the years in the Clark home and on one occasion met a music teacher engaged for Lisette and fell in love with her. Her name was Emily Calderwood. They married and for their honeymoon they traveled up the Missouri once again. He took Emily to a new falls that he discovered on one of his fur trading trips. It was not far from the ones he had named for his mother. These falls however he named Emily for the sound of its water was as musical as his bride's voice.

Life in America
in 1804

Historical Note

In early 1803, a group of events occurred almost simultaneously. These events were essential to the success of the Corps of Volunteers for Northwest Discovery. Like many other people in the United States, President Thomas Jefferson dreamed of the Northwest Passage. The Northwest Passage was said to be a river route across the continent, through the western mountains, to the Pacific Ocean. Such a route would enable ships to quickly and economically reach the new trade routes established between the Pacific Northwest coast and the Orient.

With these thoughts foremost in his mind, President Jefferson asked Congress for $2,500 to outfit a small party of men to explore the Missouri River as far as the Pacific Ocean. The expedition would seek a water route through the continent and open trade relations with the Indians. It was to be a commercial venture, seeking trading partners and trade routes, as well as a scientific venture.

At this early date in 1803, it was probable that Jefferson's proposed expedition would travel through foreign countries' land possessions. Great Britain claimed the Pacific Northwest; Spain, the Southwest and much of the West; and France, the Louisiana Territory. Jefferson asked the ministers of these three countries for passports for an expedition made up of "An intelligent officer with ten or twelve chosen men, fit for the enterprise and willing to undertake it."

In April, word came that France had agreed to sell the Louisiana Territory to the United States for $15 million. There were approximately 820,000 square miles in the Louisiana Territory. For about three cents an acre, Jefferson doubled the size of the country.

Jefferson asked his private secretary, Meriwether Lewis, to lead the proposed expedition. In turn, Lewis asked a friend, a fellow Virginian and army officer, William Clark, to share in the leadership of the adventure. Lewis wrote a long letter to Clark in June 1803. He described the expedition, and concluded his letter:

> Thus my friend you have so far as leasure will at this time permit me to give it to you, a summary view of the plan . . . If therefore there is anything under those circumstances, in this enterprise, which would induce you to participate with me in it's fatiegues, it's dangers and it's honors, believe me there is no man on earth with whom I should feel equal pleasure in sharing them as with yourself . . .

Clark's reply one month later was warm and enthusiastic:

> The enterprise &c. is Such as I have long antic-ipated and am much pleased with . . . I will chearfully join you in an "official Charrector" as mentioned in your letter, and partake of the dan-gers, difficulties, and fatigues, and I anticipate the honors & rewards . . . My friend I do assure you that no man lives whith whome I would perfur to undertake Such a Trip &c. as your self. . . .

These two men would lead the expedition for two and a half years, along a trail almost 8,000 miles in length. The success of the Corps of Discovery was based, in part, on the respect and admiration the two men had for each other. They knew and understood each other's strengths and weaknesses, and they saw themselves as partners in the "enterprise." They were friends.

Clark brought his slave, York, along with him. York was the only black member of the Corps of Discovery. Many of the other men were serving in the United States Army and volunteered for the journey.

Six men kept diaries of their journey: the two captains, three sergeants—Charles Floyd, Patrick Gass, and John

Ordway—and one private, Joseph Whitehouse. These men wrote in their journals in the rain, the wind, and the snow, huddled around a smoking campfire, and at their leisure at Fort Mandan. They wrote after a hearty meal of venison steak and on empty stomachs. They wrote when they were ill, when they were tired and cold, and when there was "joy in camp."

The Corps of Discovery spent their first winter together at Camp DuBois, at the confluence of the DuBois [Wood], Missouri and Mississippi rivers. Here, the two captains trained their new recruits and purchased additional supplies, including food, trade goods, and equipment for camping, medical emergencies, and mapmaking.

On May 14, 1804, the Corps of Discovery proceeded on, up the Missouri River. Over the next two and half years, the words, "we proceeded on" would be a familiar entry in the men's journals.

As they followed the Missouri River through the Louisiana Territory, the Corps of Discovery met numerous Indian nations. The journal pages were filled with information about the people they met: their clothing, shelter, methods of subsistence, and customs, traditions, and beliefs.

For example, on August 13, 1805, Lewis described the traditional Shoshoni smoking ceremony:

They seated themselves in a circle around us and pulled of their mockersons before they would receive or smoke the pipe. this is a custom among them as I afterwards learned indicative of a sacred obligation of sincerity in their profession of friendship given by the act of receiving and smoking the pipe of a stranger. . . .

Clark was the expedition's cartographer. He used a large, blank map to trace their route, and to fill in the unfamiliar spaces across the Louisiana Territory, the Rocky Mountains, and the Pacific Northwest. Whenever Native Americans shared their knowledge of geography with him or drew their own maps for him, Clark was careful to incorporate the information into his own maps.

The men filled their journals with descriptions of the land, the flora, and the fauna. Sergeant John Ordway described the area near the Three Forks of the Missouri River:

Some of the high knobs are covred with grass. A fiew Scattering pine trees on them. the River crooked Shallow and rapid. Some deep holes where we caught a number of Trout.

The Corps of Discovery spent their second winter [1804–1805] with the Hidatsa-speaking Indians on the Missouri River. The expedition's carpenter, Sergeant Patrick Gass, directed the men in the construction of a triangle-shaped stockade called Fort Mandan. Here, the two captains hired Toussaint Charbonneau and his 16-year-old Agaiduka Shoshoni wife, Sacajawea, "to act as an Interpreter & interpretress for the snake Indians" in the Rocky Mountains.

In the spring of 1805, the expedition departed Fort Mandan. There were now 33 people in the Corps of Discovery—the two captains, three sergeants [Patrick Gass, John Ordway, and Nathaniel Pryor], 23 enlisted men, York, three interpreters [Drouillard, Charbonneau, and Sacajawea], the infant [Jean-Baptiste Charbonneau], and Seaman [Lewis's dog].

From Fort Mandan, the Corps of Discovery followed the Missouri River across the northern Great Plains, using canoes and the two pirogues. With the help of the Shoshoni, Flathead, and Nez Percé Indians, the Corps of Discovery safely crossed the Rocky Mountains on foot. Horses they had purchased from the Shoshoni carried their food, clothing, medical supplies, and trade goods.

Safely across the Rocky Mountains, the Corps of Discovery camped along the Clearwater River, near several large villages of Nez Percé Indians. They branded their horses, and left them to the care of the Nez Percé until they returned the following spring. The men made five dugout canoes, and on October 7, the Corps of Discovery proceeded on, down the Clearwater, Snake, and Columbia rivers toward the Pacific Ocean. Sahaptian-speaking Nez Percé, Palouse, Wanapum, and Yakima Indians guided the party through some of the most treacherous rapids on the three rivers.

On November 7, 1805, as the fog lifted at the expedition's camp on the north shore of the Columbia River, William Clark wrote:

> Great joy in camp we are in View of the Ocian, this great Pacific Octean which we been so long anxious to see. and the roreing or noise made by the waves brakeing on the rockey Shores my be heard distictly.

The Corps of Discovery chose the south side of the Columbia River for their 1805–1806 winter encampment. They built Fort Clatsop near the Netul River and several villages of Chinookan-speaking Clatsop Indians. The expedition was busy that rainy winter hunting elk, making salt, clothing, and moccasins, trading with the Chinook and Clatsop Indians, and filling their journals with descriptions of the tribes they met, and the flora and fauna they had seen. Clark completed many of his maps.

On March 23, 1806, the two captains presented the fort to the Clatsop Indians, and proceeded on, back up the Columbia River, then overland through southeastern Washington to the Nez Percé villages on the Clearwater River. On the east side of the Rocky Mountains, the Corps of Discovery separated into several small parties, some to return to the supplies cached at the Great Falls of the Missouri River, some to explore northwestern Montana, and others to explore the Yellowstone River.

On September 23, 1806, the Corps of Volunteers for Northwest Discovery returned to St. Louis. Ordway described the day:

> . . . about 12 oCLock we arrived in Site of St. Louis fired three Rounds as we approached the Town . . . the people gathred on the Shore and Huzzared three cheers . . . the party all considerable much rejoiced that we have the Expedition Completed . . . we entend to return to our native homes to See our parents once more as we have been So long from them. —finis

After the successful return of the Corps of Discovery in 1806, the government rewarded the men for their work. In March 1807, Congress voted to give each man double pay and land grants of 320 to 1,600 acres. Only two members of the expedition were not paid for their services—York and Sacajawea.

Jefferson directed the Corps of Discovery to locate and confirm the existence of the fabled Northwest Passage. The route the Corps of Discovery followed was believed to be the "most practicable" route across the continent. It was not, and the dream of the Northwest Passage was laid to rest. The Corps brought back much information, including geology, flora and fauna, and the cultures of the Indian nations. For better or for worse, this information would direct the policies and plans of the United States for decades to come.

Meriwether Lewis was selected by President Thomas Jefferson to be the official leader of the epic expedition of the Corps of Discovery. Because of his success on the journey, Lewis has been called "The greatest pathfinder this country has ever known." The Lewis and Clark expedition was widely hailed upon its return and Lewis reaped the benefits of this acclaim. He was appointed governor of the Louisiana Territory in 1808.

William Clark became friendly with Meriwether Lewis when they served together in the military in 1795, and quickly accepted his invitation in 1803 to serve as co-leader of the Corps of Discovery. William Clark returned from that adventure and became a respected administrator of Indian affairs during the early years of American expansion into the West.

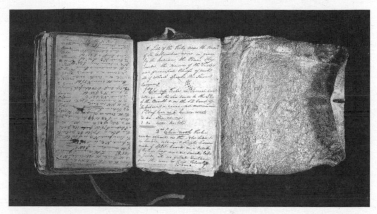

Both Lewis and Clark kept written accounts of their journey. Here is Clark's elk skin–bound journal with astronomical and altitude measurements and observations (the explorers' way of determining their exact location), from October 26, 1805. The night before, he wrote this: ". . . as it was necessary to make Some Celestial observations we formed our camp on the top of a high point of rocks, which forms a kind of fortification in the Point between the river & Creek. . . ."

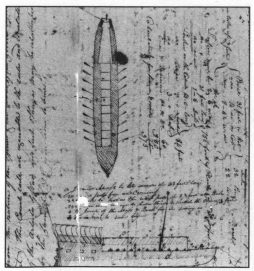

A keelboat was used for the first part of the voyage. It could be sailed, rowed, or poled along. This is a drawing from Clark's field notebook of the boat as he saw it.

The meeting at Council Bluffs was crucial to the success of the expedition, as it was the first council between Lewis and Clark and the Indians. It set the stage for the many conversations and negotiations that were to come. Noted by Clark on August 3, 1804, at Council Bluffs: ". . . our Party paraded & Delivered a long Speech to them expressive of our journey the wishes of our Government, Some advice to them and Directions how They were to Conduct themselves. . . ."

Given to various Indian leaders as a proclamation of peace, the United States peace medal worn by the Indian chief in the foreground was a treasured possession. Any Indian who accepted a medal was expected to be loyal to the United States. With the exception of John Adams, every president from George Washington to Benjamin Harrison issued peace medals embossed with his likeness on one side. At Council Bluffs, Clark wrote: ". . . we Sent him the speech flag Meadal & Some Cloathes. After hearing what they had to say Delivered a Medal of Second Grade to one for the Ottos & one for the Missourie and present 4 medals of third Grade to the inferior chiefs two for each tribe."

The Corps of Discovery spent the winter of 1804–1805 at this Mandan village. It was essential that the expedition establish good relations with the local people in order to encamp there for the winter. Upon their arrival, Clark wrote: ". . . I walked up & Smoked a pipe with the Chiefs of this Village they were anxious that I would Stay and eat with them, my indisposition provented my eating which displeases them, untill a full explenation took place. . . ."

At the confluence of the Yellowstone and Missouri rivers, Lewis put down his thoughts in his April 25, 1805 journal entry: ". . . I ascended the hills from whence I had a most pleasing view of the country, particularly of the wide and fertile vallies formed by the missouri and yellowstone rivers, which occasionally unmasked by the wood on their borders disclose their meanderings for many miles in their passage through these delightfull tracts of country."

When the expedition neared Three Forks on Monday, July 22, 1805, Lewis wrote of Sacajawea: "The Indian woman recognizes the country and assures us that this is the river on which her relations live, and that the three forks are at no great distance. This piece of information has cheered the sperits of the party who now begin to console themselves with the anticipation of shortly seeing the head of the missouri yet unknown to the civilized world."

Painting hides was an important art form of the Plains Indians. This painted buffalo robe is probably the oldest known one in existence. Lewis and Clark obtained it from the Mandans and sent it back to President Jefferson in the spring of 1805. Depicted on it is a 1797 battle between the Mandans-Minitaris and the Teton Sioux-Arikaras.

The pocket sextant was made in the late 1700s. Using a compass, a sextant, and a watch, explorers like Lewis and Clark were able to make rough maps, chart rivers, and fix their positions.

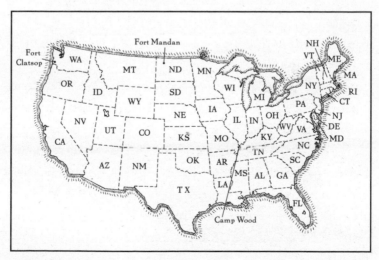

This modern map of the continental United States shows the approximate locations of Camp Wood, where the journey began, Fort Mandan, and Fort Clatsop, where the expedition finally saw the Pacific.

About the Author

Kathryn Lasky has long been fascinated by the west of the 19th century. She has written several books set in the early American west including *Beyond the Divide*, which told the story of the Gold Rush of 1849; *Alice Rose and Sam* set in the silver mining town of Virginia City, Nevada; as well as *The Bone Wars* about the first excavations for fossil dinosaur bones in the Montana and Wyoming territories in the 1870s.

"I think sometimes," says Lasky, "that I have a special gene that responds to landscapes and the landscape of the west has an incredibly strong appeal for me. Whenever I write a book about the west, in addition to the human characters, there is another character and that is the land itself . . . Imagine what Lewis and Clark must have thought as this magnificent country unfolded before them."

For Lasky to be able to write a fictional diary of the Lewis and Clark expedition was a dream come true. She had often thought of writing about the expedition but it almost seemed simply too large, too big. And Lewis and Clark were as mighty in their heroism as the powerful river they traveled.

"It would be like trying to dam a river to even attempt to tell the story of these two men. They loomed too large for me to grasp. I could never seem to get a hook into it. But then when the My Name Is America series began I realized that there could be a hook—a boy, slightly damaged by a rough and tumble life, maybe a bit frightened, but gritty and determined."

Kathryn Lasky says that "Augustus Pelletier just showed up in my imagination—begging to go on the expedition—a natural, if unfinished hero. The perfect boy for this book."

In Kathryn Lasky's mind the Lewis and Clark expedition is one of the greatest accomplishments in American History. It was not only that these men were brave, but they had wit and imagination. Kathryn found that one of the most moving parts in the entire men's journals was the occasion during which Lewis and Clark held a vote to decide on who should be Sergeant Floyd's replacement. This was not only the first election held west of the Mississippi but the first time a black man and a slave, York, was allowed to participate in the democratic process on the continent of America.

Kathryn Lasky has received many awards for her writing, including the Newbery Honor, the Boston Globe–Horn Book Award, and the *Washington Post* Children's Book Guild Award for Nonfiction. She is the author of more than forty books for children and adults, including, most recently, the Guardians of Ga'Hoole and the Wolves of the Beyond series, as well as the Daughters of the Sea books. She won a Newbery Honor for her book *Sugaring Time*, a National Jewish Book Award for *The Night Journey*, and the *Washington Post* Children's Book Guild Award for her contribution to children's nonfiction. She has also written *Marie Antoinette, Princess of Versailles*, and several Dear America diaries, in addition to two historical fiction books — *Beyond the Burning Time*, an ALA Best Book for Young Adults, and *True North* — for Scholastic. She lives in Cambridge, Massachusetts, with her family.

Acknowledgments

Grateful acknowledgment is made for permission to use the following:

Cover art by Mike Heath | Magnus Creative.

Page 158 (top): Meriwether Lewis, collection of the New-York Historical Society, 1971.125.

Page 158 (bottom): William Clark, portrait by Charles Willson Peale, courtesy of Independence National Historical Park.

Page 159 (top): William Clark's journal, ink on paper, elk skin, Missouri History Museum, St. Louis, 26081.

Page 159 (bottom): Clark's field notebook, sketch of a boat, Beinecke Rare Book and Manuscript Library, Yale University.

Page 160 (top): Meeting at Council Bluffs, woodcut, by Patrick Goss, North Wind Picture Archives.

Page 160 (bottom): *Young Omahaw, War Eagle, Little Missouri, and Pawnees*, by Charles Bird King, Smithsonian American Art Museum, Washington, DC/Art Resource.

Page 161 (top): *Bird's-eye View of the Mandan Village, 1800 Miles Above St. Louis*, by George Catlin, ibid.

Page 161, (bottom): *Junction of the Yellowstone and the Missouri*, watercolor, by Karl Bodmer, the Granger Collection.

Page 162 (top): *Lewis and Clark at Three Forks*, oil on canvas, by E. S. Paxson, mural at the Montana State Capitol, courtesy of the Montana Historical Society, X1912.07.01.

Page 162 (bottom): Robe, buffalo skin with painted detail, courtesy of the Peabody Museum of Archeology and Ethnology, Harvard University, 99-12-10/53121, 60740433.

Page 163 (top): Pocket sextant, Science Museum/Science & Society Picture Library.

Page 163 (bottom): Map by Heather Saunders.